Royally REVAMPED

FRITZI COX

Visit my website at www.fritzicox.com
Cover Designer: Najla Qamber, www.najlaqamberdesigns.com
Editor: Jovana Shirley, Unforeseen Editing, www.unforeseenediting.com

ISBN-13: 978-1-7364167-4-7

FROM THE DESK OF FRITZI COX

Dear Reader,

I've not heard any news from Penelope. The following events that transpired are pure speculation until I receive further word of her whereabouts. I will update my findings for a more enjoyable reading experience throughout the book if and when she contacts me.

In the meantime, I've stayed true to my journalistic nature and investigated *Starlight Press* and Priscilla's late husband, Loure Ankerton. I firmly believe that it's not a coincidence that Loure abruptly died—or vanished—while researching human mental health patients and their battle with a condition that caused the patients to straddle realms. To the human eye, this person was diagnosed as crazy, hysterical, or hallucinogenic. But to the fantastical creatures in the Morningwood realm, this person was only lost.

After spending weeks devouring any information I could, I came across an article from our local paper, dated around the same time as Loure Ankerton's obituary in the *Starlight Press*. The article described a mysterious John Doe patient in the mental health ward at Forks University's hospital.

He had been diagnosed as paranoid schizophrenic, yet he'd possessed an uncanny ability to practice medicine. He often performed wellness checks on other patients, confirming any missed diagnoses by the resident doctors. His knowledge and experience in the medical field had been a mystery because the man had suddenly shown up at the ward's doorstep one afternoon. For this reason, the paper called for anyone with information to come forward, as John Doe was clearly of importance to someone. The article contained a faded photograph of the man perched atop a stairwell, glaring down into the camera with tired, hooded eyes. He wore a fedora, and stitched across the right pocket of his jacket was The Council's emblem. I remembered the symbol from the old texts in Abe's shop.

I rang Forks University's mental health ward in hopes of gaining access to John Doe's medical records, claiming that I thought I was related. But the receptionist cut me off before I could ask, telling me that John was still alive, albeit a very old ninety-eight, and if I wanted to confirm his identity, I'd better hurry over. John had suffered a recent episode that left him bedridden for weeks. When I pressed for further details, she mentioned hallucinations of a woman named Priscilla. Prior to that event, he'd never spoken of her.

I'm leaving my top-secret location to meet with him today.

As always, I will report back with any news of our princess and any hopes of my ability to return to Morning-wood so that I can document the truth one hundred percent and leave the guessing to someone else. As Penelope stated in the coded article she wrote for me, I'll be the first to know of any golden vials of hope.

CHAPTER ONE

PENELOPE

I LEAPED THROUGH THE AIR, TWIRLING AND LANDING SOFTLY on my feet. Princess school had trained me in the art of ballroom dancing, but learning the grace and agility I now possessed as a vampire had been impossible in my previous state. I could glide across the ballroom like I was skating on ice and not once fumble over my heels. But even though my new body had transformed into an all-powerful machine that teetered on the edge of defying physics, I didn't feel much like dancing or celebrating my princessy qualities these days. I had been built for more.

"One more time, and then we'll move on to the repair experiment," Finn said, handing me a bottle of Project X.

I grabbed the wine and chugged it down as easily as I had during the days following my breakup with Prince Theo, except this time, hangovers couldn't touch me. Nothing could touch me. Finn and I had experimented with several different paths of pain and danger, but I still held strong and was unaffected. Just last week, we had finally tried the *big* test. I stepped into the midday sun and felt ... nothing. The Bostwick brothers had watched from inside the winery as I lay in the snow and made a snow angel while harsh sunrays beamed down on my cold, dead skin.

"I give that a ten out of ten," Grump said, shooting a forlorn glance at the empty bottle.

I wiped the back of my hand across my lips and set it down.

"What? The wine-chugging or my agility test?" I asked, pinching my nose. The scent of fresh paint, bleach, and blood would forever hang in the ballroom's air, spurring memories I'd rather leave untouched.

But as usual, I had a mission these days. And my recent trauma couldn't stop my quest for vengeance. Once The Council was dealt with, my life—or death—could finally move on.

"Both." Grump sat on his tail with a *humph.* An empty bucket of wine lay, tipped over beside him.

"Is it really necessary to send her through any more testing today? She's done her magic, given you more blood, and exercised more than any of us brothers have, put together. She needs rest." Vail's black eyes had narrowed at the mention of repair.

Each time we tested my new ability for my body to heal itself, he became agitated and alarmed with each stroke of the blade, even after my wounds swiftly closed themselves time and time again.

Finn studied me before responding. I didn't want to continue with more tests today. Ever since I'd become immortal, rest eluded me. Each night, I'd fight through cobwebs of nightmare-filled sleep. My body was a dynamic force, but I felt drained.

"Maybe if you try human blood instead of this Project X

crap, you'll have more energy." Finn stuck his chin in the direction of my wine.

It tasted like dirt, mischief, and rotten vegetables. He'd sourced it from local gnomes.

"No," I said in a firm and final voice. "That's my one rule, and I'm sticking to it. I'm still a princess and a decent person. I'm not drinking non-donated blood."

"If we could get humans to donate though—" Finn started.

"What kind of human would want to donate to our cause? Do you really think a human would support a vampire? We eat them!" Vail threw his hands in the air. His patience with his brother had worn thin ever since I'd turned.

My thoughts slinked back to Fritzi. I'd recognized her voice the moment I answered the phone weeks ago. I had tried to send her a message through Abe's bookshop as stealthily as I could and checked in with Mirror Mirror often for any signs of her even though he couldn't technically see her in the human world. If she could help me with our research, I'd learn more about my capabilities and perhaps help her return to the magical realm too. But associating with Fritzi while The Council was still a problem would only create trouble for her and her family. The last thing I wanted to do was leave her precious baby motherless.

I absentmindedly touched my palm to my lower belly and wondered what it might be like to carry a child. Fritzi's daughter, Elly, had sparked a longing in me I hadn't known I possessed. One whiff of baby powder, and my happy hormones had surged, longing for the impossible. But my womb was as useless dead as it had been alive. I couldn't bear children. I could only plant them as seeds and make a wish, and even then, motherhood wasn't guaranteed. My arms would forever remain empty. For now, cradling my pets would have to suffice. Besides, if I tried to create a Princess

Patch as a vampire, who knew what kind of monsters I might spawn?

"I can get a human. But we have to get rid of The Council first." The words wedged in my throat. "And afterward, she'd become ours to protect. All of us. Forever. I owe her. But it won't happen until the risk is zero." I straightened my spine and unhooked a hair tie from my wrist, twirling my hair into a ponytail.

Finn scratched his beard. Fatigue had settled into the pockets under his eyes. He, too, had been working nonstop since my death. But the majority of his work was in his underground laboratory, where he wouldn't permit anyone to enter, for fear that we would contaminate his top-secret lab. I had a suspicion his secrecy had nothing to do with curing vampirism despite the bottles of my pre-vampire blood "medicine" he'd brought up from his lab and tested on Drake, who had grown a steady heartbeat and weakened in response. His reaction had spooked him enough to quit my blood altogether. He questioned curing his own vampirism anyway.

"And have the other brothers come up with a plan yet? I can't create war strategies. My battle isn't on the field. It's in the lab. You know this." Finn shifted his eyes from me to Vail.

"We're meeting with Bruno tomorrow. Ian mentioned some idea with an infusion or something. I'm sure he will brief us before the meeting. I haven't spoken much with him or Drake. My battle has been with this one"—he tipped his chin to me—"and keeping her grounded during this volatile period. You know how it is to be a new vampire."

"You don't have to talk about me like I'm not here. I'd say, I've handled it pretty well so far. Besides, I'm not technically a vampire. Vampires can't do this." I waved my hand in front of his face and created a smoke screen. Tendrils of smoke curled around both of the brothers. "Or this." I turned my head toward the ceiling and formed a thunderous storm cloud overhead. A bolt of lightning struck in between us, knocking them down. My heels remained firmly planted on the floor.

"Damn! We get it, Penny! I was just saying, I want to keep you safe." Vail scrambled back to his feet.

"Seven out of ten." Grump hiccuped, falling over and sticking all four of his shaky legs in the air. "That one only singed the hairs on my chinny-chin-chin."

Finn rose back up with a groan. "You're a vampire princess. The Council won't have shit on you or us. Now, go rest. After we defeat those bastards, think of the possibilities we'll have when we're free to experiment without fear."

His eyes danced behind a sinister expression, setting off a new sixth sense I'd slowly become accustomed to over the last few weeks—intuition. I wasn't the vampire that needed to be grounded. It was Vail's mad-scientist brother, Finn, who needed babysitting.

"Come on, Little Miss Demon Spawn. Let's go to bed. The sun's nearly up," Vail said, pulling me close.

Any flicker of a heartbeat he'd once had from drinking from me had vanished. I curled myself into his empty chest and closed my eyes, willing myself to remember those bitter-sweet moments when I could hear the echo of my blood pulsing inside of him.

"Can you carry me through the halls and up into your room like old times? I can act non-demon-spawn-like. Just think of me as that dainty girl in the forest you once met. I couldn't hurt a flea!"

I raised my gaze to him, searching his eyes. His glum face turned up with a hint of amusement. My keen intuition told me it was fake.

"One, two, three. One, two—" he said.

"Three, three!" I finished as he swept me off my feet and

into his arms, barreling us outside the ballroom in a series of twirls and loops on his nimble feet.

FOR WEEKS, I'd lain in the drowsy warmth of my bed, thinking and keeping both Vail and me up with my restlessness. All the names of my friends, family, and enemies kept slipping through my thoughts, whispering me awake at night. I'd wake up, staring at the ceiling for hours on end until I drifted back to sleep minutes before my alarm dinged. My last conscious thought was always of my godmother. I'd close my eyes, reliving the pain of that final scene until I wandered into nightmare territory. The memory never faded, softened, or gave me any amount of respite. I welcomed it anyway.

But after a solid week of tossing and turning, I noticed the hollow, lifeless exhaustion in Vail's drained face and decided I needed to be alone with my thoughts and spare at least one of us from a lack of sleep. After all, we never knew when our enemies would strike again. The winery needed to remain on high alert and at full strength. The Council spared no mercy.

I stole a glance at my vampire lover to double-check his closed eyes and stealthily snuck out of bed, tiptoeing out of the room without waking him. His light-sleeping habit wasn't the easiest to work around, but the season's raging blizzard outside muffled my footsteps, so this time, I didn't need to give an excuse for leaving. Last night, I'd told him I wanted a drink, and the evening before, I'd made an excuse to check on Trevor and Otto, who still patrolled the grounds as my personal security detail.

But I couldn't hide my true intentions forever. Eventually, I would have to stop sneaking away at night to be alone and withdraw into the haunting memories I clung to like a life preserver. I didn't want to forget anything about my life before my death. Even though, unlike a true vampire, I could still feel human emotions, I wouldn't choose to forget my misery for anything. It sparked a vengeance in me that was much less Princess Penelope and much more Lady of Bostwick—the bold title the brothers had crowned me with after my birth into their world.

I needed my new ruthless persona to carry out what I had to do because wreaking havoc in the vampire world was practically signing myself up for a suicide mission.

"Another sleepless night? You're a vampire, not a zombie. Although, these days, you look like one. Jeez, lady. Ever heard of a hairbrush? How about a swipe of lip gloss? Moisturizer? Face transplant?" Mirror Mirror droned as I crossed his path in the foyer.

We'd positioned him at the front entrance for yet another security measure since, in his reflection, he could patrol both realms. Though he couldn't do anything outside of hurl insults and magic up an ugly reflection, aging his victim fifty years and scarring them for life. The first time he'd performed the trick on Ian, the cowboy had nearly thrown his boot at him.

"Never thought I'd miss your asshole tendencies, but I did." I stopped in front of him, peering back at myself.

He was right. I did look horrific. I pressed both hands over my weary, burning eyes and stretched my back, relieving the ache between my shoulder blades. Yesterday's fitness tests had taken me to the brink of my strength until I nearly collapsed under the pressure to perform. But a bottle of Project X later, and I'd stubbornly continued my training.

A hint of a smile flashed across Mirror Mirror's face, vanishing before he showed any signs of genuine care for me and ruined our playful banter. But after I'd whispered an incantation to fix the crack etched deep into his surface, we had agreed he would forever owe me. As a mirror, his image meant everything to him.

"Hardly surprised. You've always had a thing for assholes. Don't you remember all those red flags you kept bringing home to date? Like Prince Kerflufus, who had a voice like an air horn, constantly drawing attention to himself to look like the bigger man because he stood as tall as a hunchbacked dwarf hovering above an overstacked dinner plate. Or what about Edward Tickle with the tiny pickle? He had ego issues too. I caught him stuffing his pants once, you know!"

"Okay, okay! Stop!" I put my hands up in protest, but Mirror Mirror kept going.

"If I didn't know you were a princess without real parents, I would say you had major daddy issues and needed about ten years of therapy. But alas, you're just … you. No idea how you landed Vail."

"You'd better be glad I did or else you'd be in a dungeon somewhere in Troll City after Prince Theo auctioned you off. The only thing you could reflect would be hairy troll butts, green goblin farts, and your own damn ugliness."

"I guess I should thank you then. But I won't. Anyway, why are you still up?" he asked.

"You know why."

The grandfather clock chimed, echoing down the hall-way. It was noon. At this time months ago, I would sit at the lopsided kitchen table in my crumbling cottage while my godmother made tea. She had once tried to level the slanted tabletop by propping one of the shorter table legs up with a spell book. But still, Pumpkin would roll away each time she set him on the top. Of course, she would catch him before he splatted on the ground. It didn't matter now. She was gone. The cottage was gone. And Pervy Pumpkin was goo.

"Pacing the floor at night and reliving your misery won't

bring her back."

"I know. But memories are all I have left of her ... and me. I'm not who I used to be. Sometimes, I miss it. I wish I could go back to the way things were before that night. It was just easier back then. But I can't go back. It'll never be the same. I was so naive, so innocent back then."

"Innocent? Ha!"

"Well, maybe not innocent. I just have warm memories of back then. Now, all I have is cold. But I didn't have a choice. The only way to return home was to die for it. So, here I am." I looked away, staring down the hall that led to the cellar and underground laboratory, where Finn was more than likely slumbering.

"Look up, Princess. I'm only showing you this once." Mirror Mirror blurred before displaying my reflection.

I stood before him in a black dress and a golden crown. My eyes blazed with confidence, and my lips were set in a thin line of perseverance. I recognized none of it.

"That's not me. You even said I look like a zombie! Why are you playing tricks?" I stepped closer to him, peering at my regal stance.

My reflection's mood carried through the glass, jarring me and knotting my stomach. Even as a vampire, I wasn't anywhere close to the badass looking back at me. The woman before me ruled, and I was only surviving. One moment, I felt like I could take on the world, but the next, I remembered my naive-princess roots.

"This is you. This is the person we all see and the person Gertie saw too. You've been through hell, Penelope, yet you still chose the dead life, knowing its challenges. You're not a princess anymore. You're not even the Lady of Bostwick. You're a queen. You can pretend you're tough all you want, but if you were sure of yourself, you wouldn't be up at night, wallowing and second-guessing your decisions. Go back to bed and to your man. Wake up and do queen shit. We all need you. Frankly, I'm getting tired of keeping watch and seeing all these dumb humans and gnomes file in and out of the winery. Hell, yesterday, three gnomes stacked on top of each other stared into me, and the head of the bunch picked his nose for five minutes straight! I swear he tilted his head, and I could see all the way to his pea brain! I would rather be perched on the wall in an ogre's bathroom!"

"I mean, I guess I can do some cool shit these days as opposed to singing up rainbows and butterflies." I tapped my foot in front of me, striking it across the floorboards like a match and blazing a trail of fire that vanished as quickly as I'd summoned it.

"You've managed to get rid of two villains without those powers. Imagine what you can do to your enemies now. You can finish this with The Council and be on your merry way."

"I know. I just worry I'll fail and disappoint everyone. That'll be the end of curing vampirism and the end of me. And then Gertie would have sacrificed herself for nothing." I rubbed my shoulder, my knuckles kneading across my sore muscles.

My reflection reverted to my tired, true self.

"Remember when Gertie pushed you to keep practicing your spells and move forward? So you could get revenge on Theo?"

I nodded, wilting against the wall as exhaustion finally overtook me. My shoulders slumped forward, hanging limp at the base of my neck—the very spot where Vail used to love to feed.

"I don't think she was prepping you for that douche bag. She knew what you were facing. She was prepping you for this. You'd be doing her a disservice by not grabbing this new role by the balls and ending The Council."

"But I am. I train every day."

"No. Not out here." A fiery light shone over my body in Mirror Mirror's reflection before settling onto my chest like a ball of fire. "But in here."

"There's nothing there anymore." I shifted from one foot to the other.

"Good. You need to be heartless to finish what they started." His voice simmered as he showed me the confident woman again, except this time, she sat on a throne decorated with skulls, fangs still intact.

I touched the tip of my tongue to the sharp teeth in my mouth and gazed at my reflection, but the sound of snow crunching underfoot tore my attention away from our awkward bonding moment.

"Did you hear that?" I tilted my head toward the commotion.

"Hear what? All I hear is the wind," he said.

"No. It's footsteps. They're coming from the back. Outside." My voice drifted into a harsh whisper.

"Maybe one of the day workers dropped by to check on something."

"In the middle of a blizzard?" I asked.

"Should I sound the alarm?"

"What alarm?"

"I don't know. Scream?" he squealed.

"Shh! No. Don't wake anyone. I'll go check it out." I barrel-rolled across the floor with a sudden burst of paranoid energy before rising to my feet and smoothing my robe back down.

"What the hell was that?" His face drooped with distaste.

"I have no idea. It just felt right at the moment. Did I look awesome?" I asked.

"You'd better pull out your blazing toes. Otherwise, whoever is lurking at our door will only die of laughter once they see you perform that move again."

11

"Fine." I snapped my fingers and sent up a spark. "I'll be right back."

"You can't say that! Those are famous last words. You've so much to learn," he groaned.

I held a finger to my lips and disappeared down the hall. My breath caught in my throat as I neared the door to the back patio. The familiar chilled silence that surrounded me was the same as I'd felt in Priscilla's manor when she locked me away. But the sound of footsteps stopped, disappearing altogether before I looked out the window.

"Who's there?" I turned but saw no one. I paused, listening again and sharpening my senses.

A clatter rang out from the direction of the laboratory.

"Finn? Is that you?" I inched toward the winding staircase that led to the cellar and the underground lab.

Snowy footprints wound down the hall, leading toward the kitchen.

A creaking door opened and closed upstairs, followed by the familiar gait of Vail coming down the steps. I glanced behind me to see him rushing toward me. His skin singed with each pass through the sunlight filtering through the windows.

"What're you doing up? Are you okay? Mirror Mirror said you heard something," Vail greeted me with a husky whisper, panting.

A glass shattered in the kitchen. We both jerked our attention in its direction, pulling ourselves up to our full height and prickling in the notorious vampire stance—posed and ready to pounce.

"Stay here," he whispered.

I shook my head and pushed past him, but he put his hand up, stopping me.

"We need you. I need you. Stay here, and if I need help, I'll ask for it. It's probably just Drake, looking for a midnight gulp of blood." He extended his arm and gave me a commanding caress.

"What if it's a killer? I can heal myself! You can't! You're smoking, just standing near the open window!" I pried his hand free of me and crossed my arms.

He fanned a puff of smoke from his neck and made a dismissing gesture. "That's nothing. Stay here."

He disappeared around the corner before I could protest.

I quietly inched behind him, hopping on my tiptoes and holding my arms out for balance, which I didn't need. I could stand on one foot atop a broomstick and not falter—a far cry from my clumsiness in my previous form. Vail stopped at the entrance of the kitchen and scratched his head. I paused, slowly backing up in case he turned to catch me, ignoring his command.

"How did you … I thought I told you to stay back there." He stared into the kitchen.

"I am back here. I'm following orders! Sheesh," I said.

His eyes widened with alarm as he spun around to look at me.

"What? What is it?" I shuffled my feet toward him.

His eyes darted back and forth from the kitchen to me, but he only made a strained guttural sound, unable to speak.

"Vail?" I swallowed hard.

A sense of dread bloomed inside of me. Whatever sat on the other side of that wall was horrific enough to shock and paralyze my courageous and magnificent vampire boyfriend.

I shook my hand, blazing balls of lightning ready at my fingertips, and peeked around the corner.

At the far end of the kitchen, I watched myself drink from a bottle of Black Label. A cold shiver spread throughout me, dizzying my senses.

"That's me." My voice broke. I froze in the doorway, lowering my hands to my sides.

An exasperated male voice drifted from behind us.

"Fuck! Fuck! Fuck!" Finn stomped down the hall. His lab coat flew out from behind him like a cape as he echoed my thoughts entirely. "Fuck! Sorry! Sorry!"

He pushed past us, heading toward the other me on the opposite side of the kitchen, who sat, toying with her golden hair. She blew out a breath and took another sip of wine before propping her heels on the table and leaning back in the chair.

"You can't be here!" Finn hissed, jerking the woman to her feet.

The glass of wine fell to the floor, shattering to pieces. Droplets of wine as red as blood splattered across the kitchen tiles.

"Hey! You can't touch me like that!" I shouted, running to my twin's defense.

She rested a hand on her hip and squinted at Finn, posed to strike.

"It's not you! She can't feel anyway. She's … she's …" He put his hands up in defense.

"What? She can't? What do you mean, she can't feel? Is she a vampire? How did you find her?" Vail spoke to Finn but continued gazing at the other me.

"I didn't find her. I made her." Finn turned toward me. "She's your clone. Our decoy. I wasn't ready to introduce her yet."

My vision blurred as I stumbled backward into Vail, who stood equally unsteady.

"You cloned me?" I asked. I cast a sidelong glance of utter disbelief at the woman beside me.

"I had to." Finn threaded his fingers through his hair and sighed. "It's part of the plan."

"You could have asked!" I spat out in a bitter tone. My

temper flared at the thought of yet another problem falling into my lap.

My clone inched closer to Vail and winked. Her mouth parted slightly, the same way he'd told me mine did when I was in the mood. He cocked his head to the side and raised his brows. His mouth twitched, stifling a brief hint of amusement as his gaze bounced between her and me. I didn't need a superpower to read his thoughts.

"Don't you even think about it!" I pointed to my clone and then to Vail, glowering at them both.

"Relax. She won't be around long. She's only here to help us get rid of The Council, and then I'll get rid of her," Finn said. "It was just an experiment. One that wasn't ready yet, but I guess the clone's out of the bag now! Besides, she's not even technically alive. I only used a charming potion to make her appear that way. The rest is coded into her brain … badly. She's a mistake, like a malfunctioning machine. Look, she has no idea what we're talking about even! She can't speak. She's only enchanted to be like you without the magic, feelings, and words—apparently because I fucked that part up. She's a literal bag of bones with half a brain—an ogre's at that. I couldn't give her a whole one. Didn't have it on me. Don't ask."

My clone shrugged, dragging her feet back toward the bottle of wine on the table and clasping it in both hands. She brought it to her lips and turned it up, draining it entirely. A dribble of wine spilled down her chin.

I ran my palm down my face, imposing iron control over myself. A war of emotions raged within me as I watched her plunging on carelessly.

"Fuck. That's me all right," I muttered before blowing out a breath and heading back to bed even though I knew it was pointless. After staring at my own hollow self in the face and recognizing her painful existence, I'd never sleep again.

CHAPTER TWO

VAIL

DAY AFTER DAY, I LAY IN BED, AWAKE AND ALONE. PENELOPE thought I couldn't hear her leave, but I did. I watched her sneak out of the bedroom every morning, but I didn't dare disturb her. I saw the struggle in her face each time she rose from another sleepless day. Her existence as a vampire, coupled with her refusal to feed on human blood, had drained her completely. She didn't want to tell me the truth, but she didn't have to. It was written in her tense jawline and the subtle dullness of her skin that no longer flushed a dusty rose. Her eyes had grown flat and lost that spark of summer lightning that set my soul on edge. Instead, now, she stared back at me with a glassy, shadowed gaze as black as volcanic rock.

I stretched my arms over my head and quietly watched as my vampire princess slumbered beside me, finally fast asleep. Her rhythmic breathing—a human habit some vampires never broke—steadied into a lulling snore.

Our bedroom stayed empty and too quiet for my liking.

But Trevor and Otto refused to sleep with us these days, insisting on keeping watch over the winery. I didn't protest. I knew it made them feel useful. The only time one of Penelope's wayward pets warmed our feet had been when Grump drunkenly stumbled into our room, collapsed on the end of the bed, and accidentally pissed himself. After that rude awakening, we'd started locking our bedroom door.

Mixed emotions of guilt and relief surged through my veins, where her blood used to pulse, extending her lifeline to mine. The cool touch of her body no longer warmed me, and the sunshine in her veins had disappeared with her heartbeat. But my feelings for her never faltered. Whenever I looked at her, my heartless chest swelled with an emotion I'd thought was long since dead. She only needed to speak my name, and a drugging tingle would spread throughout my body, settling inside my chest like a smoldering ember.

I swung my legs off the bed and pushed myself up as softly as I could.

"Don't go." Her hand shot out, grabbing me by the wrist.

I craned my neck to look at her, trailing my gaze from her bared fangs down to her ivory shoulders and her exposed breasts. Her nipples stiffened, an innocent pink against her ghastly paled skin.

"Stay with me," she said, pulling me back down to her.

My mouth throbbed with need. We hadn't made love all week.

"You need sleep."

"I'll sleep when I'm dead."

"But you are."

"You know what I mean." She moved my hand down her thighs, parting them as she teased me back between the sheets. She felt like slick velvet.

The sound of the shower running echoed down the hall

from Ian's room, and the scent of freshly ground coffee wafted upstairs, drawing my attention to my dreaded tasks.

I groaned, pulling my hand back from her grasp despite the sweet agony of anticipation.

"I know what you mean," I said, hovering over her and pausing between kisses. "But that doesn't change the undeniable fact that you and I have a meeting with a dragon and his werewolves in a few hours. I need us both clearheaded and well rested. I can say that for me. But what about you?"

"Have I ever been clearheaded?" She sighed, pulling the blankets up under her chin.

I brushed away a lock of inky-black hair from her face, tucking it behind her ear with her golden curls. I'd noticed the darker magic she performed, the more streaks filled her hair. Each death became like a tattoo, marking her in black strands across her scalp. I wondered how long it would take for her hair to grow as entirely black as a raven's wings or the empty eyes of a demon.

"There's nothing I want more right now than to climb on top of your silken body and make love to you until we're both too tired to leave the bed. And then I'd want to do it again. But I never want to lose you like I did, Penelope. I'll do every damn thing in my power to prevent that. The Council needs to be taken care of before they take care of us first. I doubt we have much time. We're moving too slow, and they could show up here any day and wipe us all out."

Her mood plummeted.

"I've chased vengeance all year, and it's exhausted me. The Council will be my last victims." Hatred blazed in her eyes, smothering her exhaustion like a snuffed candle's flame.

"You deserve rest. I wouldn't ask you to become involved with this mess if you didn't have to be. Do you want to stay here? You can stay with … your clone. I can meet with Bruno myself and work out a plan," I said.

She rose in one fluid motion, drawing herself up to her full height until she stood fully naked in front of me, her new body carved like marble. The blankets fell at her feet.

"I want to see the vampires who conspired with Priscilla to ruin *my* night and massacre our party pay the price. They're hunting me, and I don't play with my prey. I have all these superpowers now. What else would I use them for? I'll destroy them all. Just call me Vigilante Vampire," she hissed, scraping her fangs over her bottom lip until it bled. It healed before a droplet of blood trickled down the side of her mouth.

I pushed myself up, stepping into her and searching her tired eyes. I knew there was more behind the brittle mask she wore because I wore one too.

"I prefer Princess Vampire. Besides, you don't have to be entirely evil now that you're on the other side. You can still snap your fingers and have confetti fall from the ceiling instead of, you know, fireballs," I offered.

A muscle flicked in her jaw. The hint of who she used to be lingered around her rough edges, as if she was fighting to find balance.

"I do miss the confetti sometimes," she answered, turning away from me and lifting her arms to cover her breasts. "But the problem is, I don't want to be either. I just want to be me —or whoever I was meant to be. I don't want to be Princess Penelope, searching for a white knight, or vampire Penelope, searching for her next victim. I just want my life to lead me to where I'm supposed to go, and I think that's here. I think I'm supposed to help with curing vampirism, but maybe there's more. There's so much I don't know about myself. Surely, my fate doesn't lie in an endless cycle of retribution. There has to be more to life—or death—than that."

"What would you like your life to look like?" I weighed her with a critical squint.

Whatever she wanted to tell me teetered on the tip of her tongue. I sensed the struggle as soon as she opened her mouth to speak, but then she stopped herself.

She flopped on the edge of the bed with a sigh, hugging her knees and covering her nakedness with the thin cotton sheet. Every night, she'd steal that damn sheet out from under me, wrapping herself up like a mummy until she woke and snuck away. But still, I never disturbed her. I'd let her have any comfort she could get, so I'd invested in my own bedding set, complete with a separate top sheet. Problem solved.

"I can't believe we've never talked about this," she said, reaching for my hand.

"About what?" I sat next to her, closing my palm over hers and offering a reassuring touch.

"The future. Our goals. What we want next." Her voice grew fragile, shaking.

"Well, we've never really had the time. Our relationship has been hurdling from one trauma to the next. We've not been able to focus on just us."

She jiggled her foot against the bed, thumping an obnoxious knocking sound.

"I wanted to try for a Princess Patch. At least, I think I did. Gertie and I had both dreamed of raising a princess who would learn more than the typical curriculum the princess school taught me. We wanted to teach our girl independence too. You know, like how to survive if she ever ended up like me.

"If it wasn't for Gertie sticking with me after Theo cast me aside, who knows where I would be? I didn't know anything about survival. I'd hate to see it happen to another woman—or anyone really. But my heart is with the royal girls. They wouldn't stand a chance in this world if, Goddess forbid, they encountered a dismal turn of events similar to mine. I wanted to help them. But I'm a vampire now, and that fantasy died with me."

Her mouth dipped into an even deeper frown. "That's why I think I'm restless. I had a future, and now, I don't know what I have. I'm not in the human world anymore, but I'm still lost. Turning vampire didn't fix that. I guess I thought things would be different. But, hey, check out these bitchin' abilities I have now, right?"

She rolled her eyes, sending a bolt of lightning across the ceiling.

"You're second-guessing your decision to become one of us. It's understandable—and the reason my brothers and I want to cure vampirism." I put my hand under her chin and turned her toward me. "It's okay. Turning vampire didn't extinguish your feelings, as it did us. I still … feel emotions when I'm with you. They grow stronger and stronger, the more we're together. Love and heartache. But I don't have regrets or a fond pulling to my past. I can't imagine how hard that would be."

"I miss her." She blinked back tears.

"I know. But what I'm trying to say is, you're more than a vampire cure already. You still make me feel things I didn't believe possible. And I haven't even fed off of you in ages! You might not be helping princesses, but you're changing things by helping me—and eventually, other vampires too. It's a start. If it makes you feel better, I can put on a tiara and carry a wand. You can teach me what you know." I stroked back the damp curls framing her face.

Her face brightened at the suggestion. "Can you wear a corset too? Oh, and maybe prance around in a pair of glass slippers?"

"Whoa! Whoa! Whoa! Maybe. But I draw the line at a petticoat. Otherwise, I'm game. Bring on the bubbles and pink shit." I gestured in a sweeping motion with both arms.

A burst of laughter rippled through her, ricocheting off the empty walls in our drab bedroom. My chest leaped with the tiniest of heartbeats I hadn't felt since before she'd turned.

"And, Penelope?" I squeaked out. Parched, I swallowed hard. I'd quit feeding off of her a while ago to save my strength for whatever trouble lurked in my future. My only meals consisted of Project X, and our supply was drying up faster than we could replenish it.

"Hmm?"

"I want children, too, and a future." My eyes clouded with visions of the past. Most of my memories of human life had blurred or faded—a mechanism I believed had been built into vampires for self-protection. But some of us were still left with the ache of remembering and the void of what we missed.

"You do?"

"I do."

"How?" she asked.

"I don't know. But it's one of the things I've bugged Finn about figuring out. I don't think it's impossible, especially after you gave me a heartbeat. It's basically bringing me back from the dead. Hell, you're changing me, even without your blood. It's like you have a healing aura too. Maybe all of these unique qualities you have now can help us both get what we want."

"Together?" Her face split into a wide grin.

"Would you like that?"

"I say, let's try experiment number one. Fuck the were-wolves and dragons. Actually, wait. That's not the experiment. I mean—"

"I know what you mean," I growled.

"Fuck me, not them. They can wait. Er, for you to meet

them. Not screw them." She threw the sheet off and climbed atop me. "Make love to me. I need you."

I gathered her in my arms, roughly pulling her to straddle my lap. The thought of a future together filled me with a strange inner excitement. An emotion I suddenly remembered from my time as a prince.

"I need you too," I muttered into her mouth, touching my lips to hers in a not-so-gentle possessiveness.

Her body felt like both ice and flames as I lost myself in the possibility of hope and the comfort of a new beginning.

THE CAVE HAD RECENTLY UNDERGONE renovations since the last time Penelope and I had escaped its rocky walls. After the fiasco with Penelope and the wolves, I'd doubted Bruno "The Bogeyman" would want us back. But all it had taken was the mere mention of a business opportunity for Bruno to blow a curl of smoke from his nostrils and set up a meeting. The ancient dragon loved money more than he held grudges. To him, a grievance could be quickly taken care of and forgotten in one chomp.

"You should've let me bring her. How will he believe us if he can't see Nyuk-Nyuk for himself?" Finn exited the car, slamming the door behind him.

"I still can't believe you cloned me just to kill me. The least you could do was let me name her! What kind of name is Nyuk-Nyuk anyway?" Penelope's leather pants squeaked as she slipped across the backseat and out of the car.

She'd insisted on looking as intimidating as she indeed was. Long gone were the days of ribboned corsets and pink lace. My vampire girlfriend's fashion choices dived right into the dark side. I wasn't complaining. She wore fishnets to bed.

"It's the sound she makes. You know, *nyuk-nyuk*." Finn stomped away, Penelope quick on his heels.

"Those two are like brother and sister. They butt heads more than two bulls in rutting season," Ian said, sidling up next to me.

"Yeah. She isn't happy about the clone." I lowered my voice and sighed.

"I rather like ol' Nyuky-Nyuky." Drake licked his lips, showing a sliver of a fang. "She's not entirely dumb with only half an ogre brain. She still knows … some stuff."

I stepped in front of him, cutting him off. Up ahead, Penelope and Finn both pushed past the crowd, winding through the line snaking outside of The Cave. The massive werewolf guarding the entrance didn't bat an eye as they passed.

"What do you mean?" I asked, narrowing my eyebrows at my unpredictable younger brother and studying his lean, ashen face.

He held his palms up in mock surrender but didn't break eye contact. "I'm just saying, that clone's been all over me like a vampire on fresh blood. I haven't done anything. And I won't because that'd be like banging your girlfriend. But you, on the other hand, could have fun with that, you know," he replied.

Ian blew a breath out of his nose and pulled my elbow. "Come on, knuckleheads. I reckon you can discuss the morality of banging a brain-dead clone in a ménage à trois later. We've got business to attend to." He tipped his chin toward the entrance, where a group of werewolves in suits stood, staring at our huddle.

"What morality? We're vampires." Drake shrugged, stepping around me and continuing toward the entrance.

A deep rumble of bass came from inside the cave, rattling what was left of my nerves. Between meeting with a dragon and his hairy entourage security detail, my newly birthed vampire princess with a short fuse and her nitwit clone, and my horny yet also sensical brother, I was already on the verge of losing it. The only trouble I wanted part in was ending things with The Council, so Penelope and I could move on with our future together. After she'd opened up to me about her wishes, a fiery spark of motivation had ignited within me. I had to end our threat now.

We made our way into The Cave, directed by a beastly werewolf with one cataract eye. He unhooked a rope, blocking the path down a winding tunnel, and nodded toward it. Finn and Penelope's banter echoed up ahead. I picked up my pace, catching up to them.

Finn's mouth thinned in displeasure. "I can't talk about it right now. Maybe later. Besides, you wouldn't understand if I tried to explain it."

"What do you mean? Do you think I'm stupid? Like I can't understand scientifical physics stuff? Like plants, and animals, and chemicals, and all that jazz?" Penelope's voice rose to a piercing level, sending the hair on the back of my neck to stand at attention.

"No! It's not even that. It's not that at all! It's something different. This isn't the place to talk about it. Later," he urged in a hushed tone.

"Gentlemen," Bruno said, interrupting their conversation. "And lady. Welcome." He stood at the end of the hall, pushing his hands deep into his pockets. He didn't even bother to hide his slit yellow eyes.

"Bruno!" I wound my way around my brothers and Penelope and stepped forward, greeting him first. Ever since Leo had died, the Bostwick brotherhood's leadership had fallen on me. "It's good to see you," I lied.

He smiled, displaying a forked tongue, and slowly raked

his eyes over Penelope, setting my teeth on edge. "Is it though?"

He cocked his head to the side and turned on his heels, leading us toward a long wooden table in the center of an open room. Along the back wall, etched golden double doors sat, nestled into the boulders. Two wolves stood silently, guarding the entrance to what I imagined was Bruno's lair.

"I'm sorry about Priscilla. She … well, we—" I started.

"She tried to lock me in a cage like a rat. I don't handle myself well when I'm backed into a corner," Penelope interrupted.

Bruno stopped at the head of the table and motioned for her to sit on the chair beside him. She pulled out the seat and plopped down without hesitation. I walked around the table, taking a chair across from her, opposite Bruno. My brothers all picked a spot and settled in for a prickly conversation.

"I remember," Bruno said, easing into his chair. "Your performance here and at the investor ball was … phenomenal." A puff of smoke escaped his nose, spiraling upward before vanishing.

"So, we're cool? You're okay that I killed your friend?" Penelope folded her arms across her chest and leaned back, entirely too confident in her conversation with a centuries-old dragon.

"I find you amusing, Princess." He chuckled nastily. "I don't concern myself with trivial matters. There's not a soul in this realm that means a thing to me. It's all business. I was fond of that old witch, but I was fonder of her talents in lining my pockets, which is why I agreed to meet with you. You stopped my cash flow when you stopped her. I need that up and running again. I worked with Bostwick Winery through Priscilla. I guess"—he turned toward me and sneered—"I work with you now."

He glared at me with burning eyes. It wasn't only a rumor

26

that the old dragon preferred arrangements with female partners. Bruno craved eye candy like I craved a breath of life. Lucky for him, women tended to flock to a handsome man with a basement full of treasures. And lucky for me, my cure nestled in my bedsheets every night.

Ian and Drake exchanged a nod before tipping their chins up and urging me on.

"You're correct. I took over her estate. What's left of it anyway. And I can certainly get your revenue back up and running with the winery. I'm not sure what kind of deal you struck with her, but it remains the same with our brotherhood. Our wine is yours," I assured him, meticulously weighing my words and erring on the side of giving away too much rather than too little. I knew enough about offending dragons that I wouldn't flirt with becoming his charred lunch. "But we're here for a different business opportunity. How much do you know about the laboratory underneath the winery?"

The security guards shifted on their feet.

"Your quest to cure vampirism and revert to mere humans?" Bruno raised his brows.

"Right," I said, clearing my throat and mentally cursing Priscilla.

"We found the cure," Finn said, clasping his hands together in front of him.

"Is that so? Let me guess. Ogre dung? Troll ears? Gnome polyps?" Bruno asked, his lips curled at the edges.

"Gnome polyps?" Penelope wrinkled her nose.

"It's her. Penelope." Finn flicked his eyes to her.

I drew in a sharp breath, clenching my mouth tighter.

Bruno's stare drilled into Penelope, but my vampire princess didn't flinch. Instead, she lifted her mouth in mute invitation. Bruno didn't bite.

"My blood gives breath. We've figured that out. It's the

reason The Council wanted to destroy us at the ball, and they still do. We need ... protection," she said.

"What for?" He drummed his long, talon-like nails across the table in a building rhythm, reminiscent of the death march melody the soldiers had played back in my day as a prince.

"So we can murder them." A wild look shot through her eyes.

Bruno managed a choking laugh. "You want to kill the oldest living vampires in our district? And then what? What happens when their bosses come looking for them?"

"Actually, sir, they don't have bosses. The Council broke off from The League ages ago. They've been running things their way ever since. Controlling Morningwood and everyone else in their territory. You wouldn't miss them. No one would ever even know," Finn assured him.

"How do you know their history so well?" Bruno adjusted his tie and leaned forward, resting his elbows on the table.

"I ... worked with them. Briefly. Ages ago." Finn looked away, refusing to meet my eyes.

I made a mental note to ask him about his past that he'd never disclosed. As a rule of thumb, vampires didn't talk about their former lives. But mingling with our enemies, even if decades ago, was something the brotherhood should have known about.

"They're going to kill us to stop our cause. They don't want to cure vampirism. They like being at the top of the food chain," I said, offending him as soon as I let the words slip out.

Beside me, my brothers tensed.

Bruno snapped his eyes to mine.

"I mean, they like being predators. Not at the top. Whatever. The point is, we need to kill them before they kill us.

That's where you'd come in," I continued, smoothing over my insult.

Dragons were on an entirely different level of the food chain, practically untouchable.

Penelope sat, undisturbed, toying with a lock of hair and waiting for his answer.

"What's in it for me?" he asked.

"The Council has a vault full of treasure. One of the vampires, Captain Tuttle, used to be a pirate. I think he has something you want," Ian said in a low drawl. His cowboy hat slipped down over his forehead, hiding his furrowed brow.

The dragon's eyes shone, clouding with visions of his past and confirming the rumors about his quest for Tuttle's fortune as accurate. The pirate had owned a crown crafted from the last line of Odina Dwarves—the only surviving piece of ancient magical history from them in existence.

"What's the battle plan?" The tense lines in his face relaxed as he looked between us all.

"Well, we're hoping you'll host them here for a special vampire event. We can't have them near the lab. I'll debut Penelope—actually, her clone—and we'll kill her, showing that we give up, and grovel at their feet for forgiveness. Maybe we'll even drink some human blood to prove our loyalty. But we don't have solid plans yet. If you have any other suggestions, we're all ears," I said.

"Clone?" Bruno pushed himself from the table and paced the floor, his hands clasped behind his back.

"I told you he wouldn't believe it if we didn't bring her," Finn whispered out of the side of his mouth.

"Yes, clone. Finn successfully managed to create one. She's a little rough around the edges, but we believe we can pull it off. Penelope is going to train her." I followed him with my gaze.

29

His footsteps thundered with each shuffle forward, but his gait remained as smooth as ever.

"Do what?" Penelope snorted.

I lifted my shoulder in a half-shrug and nodded my head, hoping she would agree. I could sense the barely controlled power coiled inside her; she was ready to pounce to shut me up from making any more promises before consulting her.

He paused in front of the doors to his lair and hissed, "These vampires tried to kill me at your winery, so it's only fitting that their grave will be here. I've never trusted the dead anyway."

"What happened at the winery will never happen again." Penelope raised her chin, summoning a gust of wind and blowing out the set of candles flickering atop the table in one quick puff. A clap of lightning flashed overhead, casting a blinding light throughout the cave in a blink.

A hint of amusement teased at the corner of Bruno's mouth.

"Captain Tuttle's belongings are mine. As well as whatever else is in their vault. In return, you have my protection for this event alone. I don't work with vampires. Don't make me regret this deal. It sounds like a circus act."

He opened his mouth and shot a flame directly toward the candles, reigniting them. The wolves howled in approval.

CHAPTER THREE

PENELOPE

It was just after sunset, and the winery was desolate. The constant chatter and laughter drifting up from the cellars had stopped when Vail shut down our regular wine tastings after the massacre due to safety reasons during our "renovation." These days, the only source of company we had was from visitors who came to Bostwick to buy our bottles directly. And even then, those loyal customers were few and far between. But the winery didn't need funds as it had before the investor ball. The Bostwick estate was, for once, financially stable, thanks to Vail's cunning brother.

Drake had weaseled his way into much more than Priscilla's bed when she was alive. He had access to all of her accounts as well as contacts from his role as distributor. Minus the middleman—or witch—business was booming without the overhead of entertaining. Between The Cave and the space bar, we had nearly sold out of next season's cases. Money was the least of our concerns.

Other than extinguishing The Council, my only struggle these days lay deep within the restlessness of my soul.

After my nonexistent-heart-to-nonexistent-heart conversation with Vail, I finally slept through the night, weaving my way through comforting dreams instead of torturous nightmares. I dreamed that I lay in a field, surrounded by wildflowers, staring up at the twinkling lights. Vail lay beside me, pointing out each shooting star and whispering the names of fairy godmothers we had once known. We made wish after wish until the sun came up. But we didn't need to run inside. Our skin didn't even hiss with a singe. We had been cured.

When I woke the following day, I was determined to ask Finn about the bottles of my blood he'd stored before I turned. I wanted to save a few, specifically for working on growing a Princess Patch. Without my royal blood, I couldn't complete the ritual of pricking my finger and letting it fall to the soil to hopefully sprout seedlings. It was the only way to grow a child unless I procured black-market seeds. Even then, those were extremely rare and wouldn't sprout without royal blood—if the planter was lucky.

But as my luck would have it, I couldn't even plan my dreams for the future. As soon as I'd settled into a routine, another nitwit had joined my entourage of hooligans, and another dramatic event had thrust its way into my path. So, the morning after I'd finally allowed myself to remember the scent of a baby's head or the way Fritzi's daughter had said my name with a coo, someone banged on my bedroom door and disturbed me from a heavy slumber. Reality struck again.

"I'm coming!" I yelled as I slid out of my empty bed.

The smell of magic bean water with a splash of Project X drifted upstairs. Vail was already awake.

"*Nyuk-nyuk!*" Nyuk-Nyuk called from the other side of the door.

I jammed my feet through my leggings, one leg at a time, and tied my hair in a messy bun, wishing Gertie were here to flick her wand and dress me again.

"*Nyuk-nyuk!*" she said, still banging on the door.

"Okay! I get it!" I swung open the door and stared at myself in the face.

My clone stood, half-naked, in a tattered dress, complete with a bow on her ear.

"Get in here," I said, grabbing her hand and pulling her inside the room.

I immediately went to work, straightening her outfit. If Nyuk-Nyuk was anything like me (and she was), her choice of attire fit perfectly with our personality—hot-mess city. But no one else had to know what lurked on our inside.

"Hold still!" I told Nyuk-Nyuk as I laced the front of her silken corset tight around her waist. "Suck it in, sister. Lesson one in being a princess and pulling this off is, you have to look the part. You can't walk around in Finn's lab coat and expect anyone to think you're me. Princesses don't do that type of work. We sing, dance, and look pretty."

Nyuk-Nyuk sucked in a breath and held it, purpling her face. She stared at me curiously, as if she were looking into her future. But I knew she had no future. Hell, she barely had a brain.

"*Nyuk-nyuk.*" She heaved, her bosom straining against the silken material, nearly bursting at the seams. A buzzing noise rang out loudly from her ear, as if she were on the verge of shorting out or blowing a fuse.

"I'm going to need you to say more than that too. How about we give you a proper name? I'll let you pick your own. Would you like that?" I searched her eyes for any amount of understanding.

She nodded, rocking back and forth on her heels and

shooting me a goofy grin, displaying a row of baby teeth. Finn had briefly explained why parts of Nyuk-Nyuk were more mature than others. He told me about his rapid cloning techniques, followed by patchworking parts together to—*voilà*—make me. But I hadn't understood a word he said.

"Okay, but first! Magic bean water. Have you had it yet? Of course, you'll like it. We share the same taste buds. Come on."

I led her outside of the room and down the stairs, where Finn flew around the corner, nearly knocking us over.

"You two aren't training yet? You're wasting time! What's the holdup? I need you back for more tests." He threw his hands in the air, letting them fall to his sides with an audible plop.

Nyuk-Nyuk jumped, scurrying behind me.

"We *are* training! I can't let her run around in lab coats or fraying dresses. I've been trying to dress her in normal princess clothes, so she doesn't look so damn unkempt. But some douche bag had to make my clone with an enormously freakish chest. Hell, she's got breasts the size of pumpkins! Leave it to a man to upgrade a clone. She's supposed to look like me." I rested my hand on my hip—a much less voluptuous hip than Nyuk-Nyuk's.

"I told you, I didn't have the pattern down right for creating an entirely other person. Let's just consider her chest a malfunction of my system. Besides, it looks good on her." He peered over my shoulder.

I whirled on my heels to check out my clone's other enhancements, but she had disappeared down the hall, staring into Mirror Mirror.

"I think I like this version better. She doesn't speak," Mirror Mirror yelled, his insults echoing off the walls.

Nyuk-Nyuk tilted her head at her reflection, pulling at

her eyes, ears, and nose. She turned to me in confusion, stumbling back against the wall and slumping down.

"Yoo." She pointed at me and then herself.

"Did she just speak?" Finn asked.

"I spoke too soon." Mirror Mirror gave a loud, dramatic sigh.

I rushed to her side, picking her back up by her elbow. Her arm trembled under my touch.

"Yes, you're me. We're the same. Do you understand?" I spoke each word in slow, overly exaggerated syllables.

Nyuk-Nyuk nodded.

"We're like sisters. You're here to help Finn and me."

She nodded again, clutching my arm in an iron grip.

"I thought you said she couldn't feel?" I covered my mouth with my hand and whispered to Finn, "Sure as hell looks like she feels fear."

"Nonsense. It was her natural ogre-brain reaction. They're always on the defense. Besides, she's wired and charmed to avoid feelings. I wrote the code myself," he said.

"And when she hid behind me? From you?"

"I'd kept her in the lab, tied up for a very long time. Of course she associates me with something unpleasant."

"So, all this time, you've been hiding her in your secret lab. No wonder you were weird about us going in there."

I brushed Nyuk-Nyuk's trembling fingers aside and gave her a reassuring pat. She wandered off, strolling down the hall in a series of loops and twirls I'd taught her earlier.

"I wasn't weird about anything. I just don't want my experiments tampered with—or worse, completely broken. I've spent my entire career tinkering with this type of work. It's crucial for me to get it right," he spoke with a calm authority while avoiding my gaze.

"You mean, the time you worked with The Council? Why

didn't you mention that before our meeting with Bruno? I'm sure Vail would have liked to know."

"It's a time in my life that I don't like to talk about. Besides, it offers no value to our current situation."

"I bet it does. You have insider information on them."

"Hardly. I only interned for them briefly as a lab assistant when I was working my way through school. That's it."

"Tell me about them."

"What would you like to know? They're a gang of ruthless vampires who dabble in ruthless shit. Trust me, you don't want to know any of those details. Just know they're extremely stubborn and they don't take no for an answer. They don't follow anyone's orders, especially women. They despise women."

"Wait, what? Despise women? Why?"

"They're … old-school vampires. They believe women shouldn't be in positions of power and that they're only for pleasure. They'll never turn a female if they can help it. They either feed on them or fuck them. They're from that unfortunate era where a woman's place was at home."

"No wonder they hate me. A powerful woman who can kill them is their worst nightmare. I had no idea The Council consisted of only men. What about The League you mentioned?" I asked.

"The League was too mainstream for them. That's why they broke away. There are female vampires who are higher up the chain than anyone in The Council. Leave it to the Podunk Morningwood vampires to think they could restructure our entire governing body. The only reason The League has left them alone is because they know the vamps around here are too small and too dumb to be a threat. But if The League found out about you, well, that's a whole new problem. One that, I'm sorry to say, wouldn't end well. They're entirely too big to defeat."

"We have to get to The Council before they inform The League. Damn it. We have even less time than I thought. I saw the cruelty in that vampire's eyes back in Abe's bookshop. They're going to destroy me."

"Yes. However, they'll have fun with you first. That's why" —he tipped his head to Nyuk-Nyuk—"she's crucial."

"So, you're really going to send her in there for them to torture and kill? Like a sacrifice?" The question felt like a stab through my empty chest.

"Moooom," Nyuk-Nyuk said as Grump trotted past her. Startled at her own voice, she glanced up to find Finn and me watching her with a wide-eyed expression.

"No, ma'am! I'm not your mama. I'm a goat. Look. I got a scraggly beard and balls that hang to my hooves. I'm not even a lady goat. Just a drunk one." Grump hiccuped, galloping away and out of sight, nearly head-butting every wall.

Mirror Mirror sniggered.

Nyuk-Nyuk put a hand to her throat and tried to speak again, "Mowma."

A shadow of alarm crossed Finn's face before he quickly recovered.

"It's for the cause," he muttered, spinning around and leaving before I could respond.

I watched him go before returning to Nyuk-Nyuk. A stab of guilt lay buried in my chest as my half-witted clone evolved into something much more than a bag of bones. She was just like me—lost and confused about who she was through no fault of her own.

I motioned for her to follow me, putting my arm across her shoulders and comforting her.

"No, not Mom. But I can tell you about Mom. Or my mom. Godmother actually. But let's get back to your name first. I don't think Nyuk-Nyuk fits you anymore. How about Diana?" I asked.

She recoiled, stopping in her tracks.

"Anastasia?"

She tapped her chin and weighed the question before shaking her head.

"Kate?"

She took a step back, crossing her arms over her breasts, which were spilling out of her corset.

"Garona," I tried, remembering a famous ogre name I'd once heard long ago.

Nyuk-Nyuk hopped up and down on her toes, nodding as I noticed a look of enthrallment mirrored in my own face. She performed the same happy dance I did when someone offered me a glass of wine.

"Garona it is then," I said. "Now, let's go to the ballroom and practice before Finn decides to come back and ruin the mood. I'll tell you about Godmother while we walk."

She picked her skirt up and curtsied, nearly bending herself in half. I was never that flexible.

"Whyen." Her voice came out in a low, guttural sound. She paused before coming up for air.

"Wine?" I asked.

She beat on her chest with balled-up fists and growled like a forest creature in heat. I'd heard that sound once when I caught two centaurs rutting back in Poppycock. I'd never seen anything like that since in my life—or death.

"Did somebody say wine?" Grump appeared out of nowhere, circling our feet.

His fur brushed against my shins, sending an unbearable itch throughout my cold, dead legs. I reached down, digging my nails into my flesh and shooing him away. Up ahead, Otto and Trevor waited at the back door. The gargoyle flapped his wings, sending Trevor's shedding fur flying in the air. Otto sniffed a strand up his large, open nostrils and began to sneeze while simultaneously passing gas. Mirror Mirror fogged his glass in shame, expressing his distaste for our family.

I hung my head and groaned. Any fantasy of normalcy anytime soon was a pipe dream.

"If I were still a princess, I'd have a real army. But I guess this group of misfits will have to do," I said to myself as I continued toward the ballroom one less than confident step at a time.

Outside, the moon nestled in a cloudless sky, reflecting a wispy dull light off of a layer of fresh snow.

"Come here, Garona," I called as my clone skipped ahead, holding Otto's hand and crunching through the powdery snow underfoot.

With my gargoyle's half-brain and hers, they made one whole dumbass.

Garona stopped, swirled on her feet, and dutifully obeyed my order. Along with altering my clone's figure, I'd learned Finn had also modified my stubborn streak by removing it entirely.

"Look up there." I pointed to the night sky. "Godmother watches us from up there. She would've liked you. She had a soft spot for the ... odd."

Trevor tossed his head up and let out a howl he'd learned from the werewolves. Otto tried to mimic his fox friend but instead let out a burp. Grump didn't bother stopping. He continued toward the ballroom and the wine. In the distance, an owl hooted back.

Garona stared at the stars and opened her mouth wide, letting out a ghoulish hoot, followed by a loud burp.

"That's not what that means. They were calling out in mourning. Godmother is gone now, but she used to be here." I pointed to the ground and gasped.

Beside us, a pair of fresh footprints trailed through the snow, leading to the barn.

"Heeer." She reached down, grabbing a handful of snow and letting it slip through her fingers. "Gawn." She lifted her empty palm to the sky.

"Something like that," I whispered, holding up a finger. "Wait here. Trevor, Otto, guard her."

They hopped to us, circling her feet and snarling. I stood quietly, tuning all of my senses toward the night. A cockroach with twitching antennae crawled up the side of the winery behind us. Wind snaked through rows of dead vines in the vineyard. The scent of decomposing wood and burned leaves drifted from the forest. I shook the thought of Gertie from my head and continued listening for signs of danger. But the night was as silent as my footsteps as I made my way toward the barn on nimble feet. I glanced behind me, making sure my friends hadn't followed.

I tiptoed through the backyard until I made it to the barn door. A splattering of fresh blood stood out against the stark white snow, stopping at the threshold. I swallowed the fear clawing through me and inched open the door, peering inside. My fingertips warmed with electric energy buzzing through my veins.

A clattering of metal rang out from inside the barn, followed by a string of curses. I opened the door further, spotting Drake and Ian standing next to a human man tied to a table. The man rapidly blinked, staring up at the ceiling. I could hear his rapid heartbeat from the other side of the room.

"It's working!" Ian shouted, clapping his hands together before picking up a glass of blood and drinking.

My nostrils flared. The urge to feed hit me full force. Since I'd turned, I had successfully avoided real human blood and limited myself to only Project X. The thought of drinking from a human sickened my stomach. But the scent of *fresh* human blood lulled me into a frenzy I'd not felt before.

I stepped inside and slammed the door behind me, struggling to keep my fragile control.

"What's working?" I asked, baring my fangs.

The man turned his face to me and screamed. The heat radiating from his warm body felt like sunshine against my skin.

Ian and Drake rushed toward me, blocking my path. A bitterness filled my mouth as I hungrily fought past the brothers, easily overtaking them and swatting them aside. Bolts of lightning crackled off of my skin each time they tried to restrain me, and for a slight moment, time slowed enough for me to arrive closer to their victim, untouched. But I brushed that mystery away and chalked it up to my swift movements.

"Penelope! Stay there!" Ian pleaded as I drew nearer to the man. His voice grew distant as I zoned in on my prey.

The sweet, metallic scent of the man's blood had already provoked a tingle on the tip of my tongue.

Drake groaned, holding his shoulder and struggling to get back on his feet. Vail and Grump, followed by Garona and the gang, burst through the door behind me.

"Penelope!" Vail shouted, running to my side and grabbing me around the waist. He turned me around to face him. His eyes blazed down to mine. "You don't want it! I promise! Remember? Focus! One, two, three. One, two, three, three!"

He pulled me to him tight. I strained against his arms, unable to focus on his distractions.

"He's one of us! He was a vampire! He's cured!" Drake yelled above the commotion.

My throat clenched. The magnetic pull I had toward this

helpless man evaporated as the shock of discovery throttled me.

I stopped fighting against Vail and hurtled back to reality, instantly awake and fully aware of my surroundings. The dull ache of hunger that had gnawed through my chest disappeared. I faltered in the sudden silence engulfing the room. If what Drake had said was true, I stood, staring at the first fundamental transformation in the history of ever.

"Explain." My voice cut through the silence.

I stared at the man in astonishment, picking up a familiar chill as his blood ran cold. My skin prickled as the warmth wavered inside his body.

"We've been working on a plan B. In case, you know, she doesn't work out." Ian tipped his cowboy hat at Garona and dusted his palms down his pants.

I pulled away from Vail and trailed my gaze from Ian's filthy, mud-caked boots to his tattered jeans, decorated with dirt and wine stains.

"We made a batch of moonshine and infused it with your blood. Gabe just so happened to be at the right place at the wrong time. So, he became our volunteer. It wasn't too hard to talk him into drinking the entire bottle. We just told him it shimmered from the fairy blood we'd put in it."

"You turned me human," Gabe spoke in a British accent. His voice grew heavy with malice. "Now, bite me and return me to the dead. I didn't sign up for this."

"Silence," I commanded.

The man's heartbeat pulsed in my ears. His breath quickened as I drew nearer to him.

"Please let me go. I promise I'll change. I won't do the things I used to do anymore. Please!" the man pleaded, lifting his wrists against the restraints. A long wrinkle cut deep through the center of his eyebrows.

I sensed a familiar evilness inside of him that reminded

me of the day I'd met the demon in the woods. I had the same eerie feeling as when I'd entered Morningwood Manor.

"What does he mean, he won't do things? Where did you two get him? And why the hell did neither of you notify me about this little experiment?" Vail hovered beside me, protecting and restraining me all at once.

"I picked him up." Drake stepped forward and rolled his shoulders, massaging the growing bruise I'd given him. "I know him from when I worked with Priscilla. You might think I did her dirty work, but this one here does the work no one else will touch." Drake turned to me. "I'm not able to tell you what he did, Princess. Those things shouldn't be repeated. I need you to trust me on this. The man you are looking at is—"

"Part demon," I finished his sentence, flicking my eyes away from the man's gaze.

One quick look into his empty eyes, and I had seen every disgusting thing he'd done. Drake didn't have to explain anything. I clenched my hand, puncturing my palm with my fingernails.

"How did you know?" Vail asked.

I glanced behind me. Garona and Grump were huddled in the corner. Trevor and Otto stood in front of them, posed to strike.

"I don't know." I lowered my voice and closed my eyes, concentrating on blocking out the memories scrolling through my mind from the demonic man on the table.

He threw them at me like projectiles, baiting my new weak-willed temper. I gasped, forcing the memory of a young princess lying in a pool of blood out of my head. I recognized her as Princess Peony, who had gone missing my senior year. I squirmed under the weight of his memory, watching her through his vacant eyes. He stood, satisfied, hoisting her ankles up to his waist and dragging her lifeless body through the mud behind him. A row of wildflowers sprouted and quickly withered in her wake.

She'd been a vibrant young woman, studious and kind. One day, when I'd forgotten my spell book, she'd shared hers. But she was too shy and quiet to build a friendship, often going off on her own during teatime. I was too distracted to bother with mingling. The day she went missing didn't mean much to me. Instead, I'd spent my youth chasing frogs of the non-marrying kind, quickly forgetting about the lost Princess Peony. I couldn't even remember her name.

I tucked the thought away and opened my eyes to catch him watching me. The knowledge of his crimes twisted my insides.

"She's a reader." The man's expression held a note of mockery. "Can't handle my past, can you, lady?" He opened his mouth wide and let out a bloodcurdling cackle.

Vail stepped forward and crushed his knuckles into the man's nose, knocking him unconscious before turning his attention to Ian.

Ian put his hands in the air, backing away from us both.

"We didn't tell anyone because we knew you'd protest against these trials. But we didn't have a choice. We believed we could create the cure with our products and sneak them into vampires to test. We've only ever used shitbags like this one." He cocked his head toward the man.

The human stirred, waking with a maniacal laugh.

"What kind of vampire are you that you can't handle a little blood and gore? Was it the kid you saw? Or that home-less man? Ah, I bet it was the princess who ran away from Priscilla. She didn't get very far, did she? I got a hefty prize for that little stunt. Is that what's got your tongue? Which one gave you that terrified look in your eyes that I love so much, darling?" His lips thinned in malice.

I leaped through the air, landing atop the man in a swift

and violent reaction, suddenly anxious to escape his disturbing presence. The man's eyes grew wide as I pushed my knees deep into his collar, smothering the breath out of him with each snap of bone. He began to scream, choking on his blood. A thrilling rush of bloodlust burst inside of me, shocking me senseless.

"I didn't mean it. I was just joking! I was trying to have a little fun. Please. Have mercy on me!" he cried out, peering around the room for help. A dribble of red slid out of the side of his mouth.

"No." The tight knot growing within the walls of my chest begged for release. I curled my fingers around his neck and twisted, cracking his spine. I exhaled a sigh of relief.

Visions of the ghosts he'd created escaped with his last breath. The wispy child waved good-bye before disintegrating in the wind and going to his place of rest. The peony curtsied.

I skimmed the room, looking to anyone else to explain what had just happened or confirm I wasn't dreaming. But there wasn't even a blink of distraction toward the apparitions. All eyes remained uncomfortably on me.

"Yep, you're a vampire all right. Anyone who can be that ruthless ... maybe we should send you straight to The Council. They'd not stand a chance." Ian stepped up to the table, helping me down.

Vail stood motionless, studying me for any signs of shock. I had none.

"If you had seen what I saw, you would have ended him too," I told him, shuffling out the door, passing the horrified faces staring back at me. I was too exhausted and confused to talk about my reaction to a world of knowledge they couldn't see. "I think I'm going to lie down now."

"Wait!" Vail called behind me, stopping me in my tracks.

"Drake, Ian, take care of Nyuk-Nyuk and the gang. I'll deal with this moonshine mess in a bit."

"Her name's Garona," I corrected him.

My clone lifted her chin to the room. My confidence was catching.

"Okay. You two take care of Garona and the gang. I'll be back in a bit." Vail pressed his palm to my lower back and guided me outside.

We didn't speak until we reached our bedroom.

"I'll draw you a shower really quick and then head back to deal with whatever the hell they've been toying with down there," he said, locking the door behind him.

I plopped down on the edge of the bed and nodded. I needed to be alone with my thoughts. The shower knob squeaked from the other side of the wall as Vail dialed it up to the scalding temperature I liked. I could grow used to the power that came with vampire life, but the constant chill that ran through my dead veins was pure torture.

"Do you want to talk about it?" he said, emerging from a cloud of steam. His dark eyes softened at the sight of me.

"I saw things I wish I could unsee. I didn't know I could do that. It just happened. But that wasn't even the worst part. It was the relief ... and maybe even a little bit of thrill I had when I took his life in my hands. I don't feel any remorse." I drew an invisible pattern on the blanket, distracting myself from overthinking about the way time had stopped for a brief moment in the barn. I already felt drained enough.

He took two strides toward me and sat down on the bed, lifting a hand to brush my hair behind my shoulder. The tips had grown pitch-black. I looked up at him with effort, unable to give the most important person in my life the sunshine he so clearly, desperately longed for. I needed more time to erase my pain. His smile faded a little when he realized I had withdrawn back into my grief.

Earlier, long-overdue happiness had bloomed inside me when I thought about building a life with Vail after dealing with The Council. After our conversation about the future, my heart leaped with possibility. But all it had taken was one bloody trigger to send me back to the new me and the task at hand. I couldn't think of blossoms and babies after I crossed the threshold to the other side of life. I'd chosen Vail, and I'd chosen death. Now, I was reaping the consequences.

"You're a vampire. That bloodlust will always be there, simmering under the surface. The important thing is, you didn't give in to it for the wrong reasons. From my perspective, you ended someone who needed to die. Most vampires just kill whatever and whoever. You had the sense to make a choice. You're different, and you're still learning your capabilities. Give it time and don't be hard on yourself. We're immortal! We have all the time in the world to heal. And I have patience. Healing is one step forward and two steps back."

"Who would have thought after you found me, I'd still be so lost?"

He stretched his arm across my back, resting it on my shoulders and squeezing me into him. "We'll figure you out. If you have the qualities of a princess, a vampire, a witch, and a reader inside of you, I wonder what else you can do. You know, gnomes have some useful abilities too. They can burrow into the ground. You should try it." He turned to me, easing into a smile.

"What good would that do?" I asked.

He shrugged. "I dunno. Let's try it."

I stood up, firmly planted my feet on the thin rug beneath me, and mentally pushed myself through the floor. Nothing happened. I stomped my feet, twirling in a circle, as if I could drill my heels into the wooden floorboards, but still, nothing happened.

Vail burst into a fit of laughter, lying back on the bed and clutching his sides.

I turned my back toward him and crossed my arms, hiding my smile. I would turn myself into a dung beetle if I could coax that kind of response out of him again. After the Bostwick Massacre, these gleeful moments were rare and few and far between.

He came up behind me, locking his arms around my waist. The shock of his touch still ran through me after all this time. When he spoke again, his voice was warm and his grin genuine. "Nice try, but let's stick to useful tricks. Maybe you can practice some tomorrow when you're training Garona." He kissed the back of my head.

I turned around, winding my arms inside of his jacket and around his back, pulling him into me tight. I rested my head on his chest, but the pulse I'd once felt—my pulse—was gone.

"About that. You can't let them kill her. She feels now, Vail. Even Finn saw it. She's not a robot, or a zombie, or whatever the hell he wishes she were. She's real. She's me. I don't want her as a sacrifice. If you think you can use her as a decoy, fine. But don't get her murdered. The moonshine should work just as well. Once those bastards revert to humans, you can easily snuff them out. Hell, let Garona take one too. I hear they hate women."

"I'll make sure she strangles them with her crown then."

"Promise you won't let her die? I wish you'd let me go."

"You have my word. But I can't let you go. You're too valuable to the cause and me." His voice grew smooth, insistent.

"Then, what can I do? I have all of this power. Let me help you."

He tilted his head toward the ceiling, weighing the question. The steam from the bathroom had slowly been filling the room, creating a stifling, sticky air.

"Start working with Finn on those extra bottles of blood he took from you while you were still a princess. Let's see if we can somehow grow a Princess Patch but not. Does that make sense?"

I shook my head, pretending those bottles and babies hadn't been on my mind since we'd last spoken. I didn't want to get either of our hopes up.

"You know how humans can create life before they implant life? I believe they call it in vitro. Well, I've been thinking, and Finn already created life from ... well, body parts and who knows what?" He recoiled. "Maybe we can figure out how to create royal life from your old blood. Maybe we can have a *happily ever after* fairy-tale ending. I can be your Prince Charming, and you can be my queen."

"But that's after we deal with The Council. There's no sense in starting yet," I said more to myself than to him.

"The Council is being dealt with." His voice cut sharp. "You can get a jump on the future now."

"And if something goes wrong? And The Council isn't dealt with?" I clenched my jaw, stifling a sob in my throat. The thought of an eternity without Vail painfully froze in my mind.

"I have a dragon in my back pocket. I'll bring you their charred remains if you'd like."

"I'll toast the moonshine to that."

"There's an idea! Although what kind of vampires drink moonshine? That must have been Ian's hillbilly idea. I think I'll have him alter it into white wine. Something golden, like sunlight. What will we call our new beverage?" He jerked away, holding me by the shoulders and staring down at me with a mischievous grin.

"Royal Blend," I said.

"Perfect! I can taste the sunlight already. How about a dance toward the shower?"

He bowed, extending his hand. I curtsied, taking his palm in mine.

"One, two, three. One, two, three, three." I swayed as he spun me into the bathroom to wash away the agonizing maelstrom of haunting thoughts that had muddied my path to freedom.

CHAPTER FOUR

VAIL

I POURED A SPLASH OF PROJECT X IN MY COFFEE AND GULPED it down before heading back to the barn to deal with the mess my brothers had created. But first, I had to keep my promise to Penelope and consult with Finn about Garona. The sheer look of fright in Penelope's eyes over the potential loss of her twin had set my fangs on edge. If I could save my princess from more heartache, I would do whatever it took. The struggle in her weary eyes had been evident. She needed peace and a chance to grow into her new role as a vampire. But instead, we had been thrust from one dramatic event to the next, barely recovering before we faced a new trauma.

I set my mug in the sink and stared out of the window into the black night, stalling my next move. Lately, Finn had been disappearing into his secret lab even more so than usual. These days, I rarely saw him unless he was barking orders at Garona and Penelope. He shrank away from the brotherhood and lost himself in his work, citing the importance of the cause. But we'd found the cure for vampirism, yet he still stayed underground and mysteriously quiet.

I arched my back, stretching my hands overhead toward the ceiling. I paused, listening for any signs of Penelope upstairs. I desperately hoped she was napping. I suffered through a dull ache of desire to crawl in bed next to her, but between the two of us, one of us had to make sure we were well rested for the trouble ahead. I eyed the pot of coffee, contemplating a second dose, but the moon hung low in the sky, signaling that I had better get a move on it.

"Vail! Is she all right? I heard she killed a demon!" Mirror Mirror stopped me before I could pass.

I checked myself in his reflection, shoving my messy hair away from my face and trailing my fingertips over my gaunt jawline before rubbing my puffy eyes and replying, "How'd you hear that?"

"Nyuk-Nyuk—er, Garona! Well, I'm assuming she meant demon. She pointed to herself and did a little twirl, just like Penelope. Then, she hissed, burped, and slid a finger across her throat, saying, 'Doodoomon.' " Mirror Mirror replayed the scene for me in his reflection.

"Jeez." I slapped my forehead. "She's all right. He was a test subject—and a demon. She snapped his neck like a candlestick, crushing his bones in her dainty hands. But she surprisingly took it well."

"I knew she would. She's tough. But smart. She's going to rule the world one day. I just know it. She's got that perfect balance of empathy without sacrificing her boundaries. I think her heart stopping was the best thing that could have happened to her. She was sunshine then, but she's fire now. Just don't tell her I told you that. I wouldn't want to give her a big ego and let her think I cared," he said, clearing his throat and calming himself.

"I'll tell her you said *fuck you*. I've got to find Finn before sunup. I'm sure he will want to know about all this mess." I spun around, shaking my head at the playful yet hateful relationship between Mirror Mirror and Penelope.

"Yes, tell her that! That's more my style. Thanks! And tell Finn to lay off the Madderall! He's been looking like Dr. Loony lately! He'll have us all as programmed robots before too long. Cut your heads off and program you with a foot for a face or a big toe for a nose. Something like that!" His voice died away the farther I sped down the hall.

Before I made it to the lab, I heard loud tinkering and a string of curses. Whatever mood my brother was in, I didn't want to disturb him. But my mission couldn't wait, and neither could Garona's fate. If it were up to my brother, she'd walk in as a sacrifice, and that was that. He was as heartless as the rest of us—it came with being a vampire.

Even though I knew Finn wouldn't personally harm a fly, I always had a suspicion about his true intentions to cure vampirism. He'd never once mentioned his past, but the enthusiasm he showed for our cause was telling. He wanted more than a cure. Finn was after something else.

"Finn?" I tiptoed into the lab and peeked around the corner into his office.

Paper towels lay in a pile, soaking up an oozing green liquid on the floor. A dozen empty bottles of Project X lined the top of his desk.

"What is it?" He threw his hands in the air in an explosive movement.

I bared my fangs.

"What the fuck has been wrong with you lately?" I stepped inside his office and slammed the door behind me. The vials of blood in the cooling chamber next to us rattled on their shelves.

"Sorry! Sorry." He fell into his chair and rested his head in his hands. "I've got a lot going on. It's not easy, finding the cure for vampirism, making clones, dodging The Council."

"Clones? Is there more than one?" I asked, walking to the chair on the other side of his desk and collapsing into it. I tugged at my shirt collar and leaned back. I couldn't handle any more Penelopes. I already felt Garona needed constant supervision that no one around here had the time to provide.

"No. Not clones." He waved his hand in the air, as if he could shoo the thought away. "You see those vials of blood on the top shelf?"

I nodded, drawing my leg up and tucking my foot underneath me. Something told me that I'd better make myself comfortable.

"Those four vials are all we have left of Penelope's blood before she turned. I had five, but one is missing, and I can't find it. I need it. It's all we have! We went through too many in our trials. Her blood isn't pure now."

"But it still works, right? To cure us?"

"Her pure blood, yes. But her vampire blood, no. Well, not entirely. It alters us, but to what extent, I have no clue. I haven't had time to run proper tests on her blood now. It keeps changing. The DNA re-sequences itself every few days. I never know what it will do next." He impatiently shuffled through a stack of papers. "I've run every test imaginable, all documented here, yet I can't find a damn rhyme or reason to her. I've never seen anything like it before. If we want any hope of curing ourselves, we have to stop the trials and save those last four vials, or she needs to turn herself back ASAP."

I swallowed hard. No hope for curing us also meant no hope for a future family with my princess. And after all this time, I had to give her what she wanted. She deserved it.

"About that ..." I uncrossed my legs and leaned forward. "I think I know where the fifth vial is. Ian and Drake performed some *tests* of their own ... under the radar. They mixed Penelope's royal blood with moonshine and forced some demon vamp to drink it, and he turned human. Then, Penelope killed him. So …"

"Wait, what?" A cold expression settled on his face. "They stole the blood to use it as a *mixer?*"

"I know; I know. But it worked. They hadn't needed to inject it or anything. He drank the entire bottle and changed."

Finn pushed himself back from his desk and rose, pacing the floor.

Drake and Ian burst through the door, clamoring over each other. A look of sheer terror reflected on their faces.

"It's tomorrow. We just heard word from the wolves. Bruno's hosting the meeting tomorrow!" Drake's voice came out strangled. A glimmer of youth from the blood he'd consumed radiated just beneath his surface.

Finn took in a sharp breath.

I held up a finger, stopping his verbal assault before he could release the burst of anger I sensed swelling up inside of him. The look in his eyes alone chilled my soul.

"We knew this was coming. We just didn't know it would be here so quickly," I said before anyone else could speak. "The last thing we need to do is panic. So, let's all sit down and hash this out. We'll need to prepare, and everyone has to be on the same page. Otherwise, this won't work." I flicked my gaze to Ian and Drake before letting it fall on Finn. "That means, no secrets. If you want to test Penelope's blood in moonshine, fine. But let us know what's going on. If you want to make a damn clone out of Penelope's blood, fine. But for fuck's sake, give us a warning ahead of time, so she doesn't stumble into her damn twin and shock herself."

The brothers avoided my gaze.

"I realize tensions have been high since we lost Leo in the massacre. But we won't get anywhere, running off in different directions. The recent decisions everyone made should have been discussed as a family. We're Bostwick, and we're all in this together, whether we like it or not. Our mission has been to cure vampirism. We won't let anyone get in our way of that—especially The Council. So, sit your asses down, and let's figure this out."

Finn dragged his feet back to his seat, Ian leaned against the wall, and Drake pushed himself up onto the top of a nearby table.

"What's the plan?" Ian asked. A bit of dry blood clung to the forever five o'clock shadow above his lip.

"We send in Garona. If that doesn't work, you can serve your moonshine. But good luck serving that shit to The Council," Finn said.

"We can't send in Garona as a sacrifice. She feels now. Penelope told me so." I threaded fingers through my hair.

"He's right. We can't kill that girl, no matter how dumb she is. Hell, I've fucked women without brains before, and Garona is at least somewhat coherent. There was this zombie once—" Drake started.

"Stop. Stop. We get it." I waved his words away. "We can have Garona there as a decoy, not as a sacrifice. We can let them think they can have her. But we serve the poison first. It just needs to be in wine, not moonshine. That's not our brand, and they'll be suspicious."

"You think The Council won't already be suspicious? Bruno is inviting them to a dinner meeting with us. When has that ever happened? They'll be on high alert." Finn drummed his fingers across his desk. "I don't know what went wrong in Garona's programming, but she still isn't even alive. It's all charms and codes. I specifically created her for this one event."

"Well, get it out of your head. She isn't dying. Not on my watch," I said.

"We don't have many choices at this point. I say, we go on

in there and beg for forgiveness, so they'll let us be. We tell them about Penelope and hand Garona over at the end—after they drink the wine and begin to turn. Then, we destroy them before they have a chance to touch her." Ian pushed his back off the wall and walked over to the desk, pressing his palms into it and leaning forward.

"And what if that doesn't work?" Drake asked.

"We have a dragon," Ian said, looking over his shoulder at him.

"He was here last time, and they still managed to kill a ton of guests." Finn sat back in his chair, defeated. "Penelope—the real Penelope—can destroy the entire cave. Why can't you sneak her in the back and let her stay there if something goes wrong?"

I slammed my fist on the table. "She's not going to be anywhere near the same damn vampires who are hunting her down. She's too important—and yes, that means to me, but all of us as well. She's one of us now. We're all Bostwick. Even Garona. We don't send anyone to the slaughterhouse, except our enemies. Finn, you're staying here with her." I put my hands up, stopping him before he could protest, but he abruptly stood up, knocking his chair back.

"How am I supposed to explain her DNA and genetics and all that shit I need to say to sound convincing to The Council? You don't know all of that!" He threw his hands in the air and marched around the room.

"She needs someone here. You two are Bostwick's most important assets. You can brief Drake on anything he needs to know while he works with Ian on the wine tomorrow. You know he can convince anyone of anything. He's a con man, for fuck's sake. Now, I'm done discussing it. Everyone, get some sleep. Tomorrow night is going to be brutal." I planted my heels on the floor and pushed myself up with a groan, suddenly missing Leo.

It was never in my blood to become a general. The thought of sending my loved ones off to battle sickened my stomach. Even as a prince, I'd avoided talks of war and threats from my enemies. But I had enough loyalty and honor that I couldn't let Leo's death be in vain. He'd protected the cause, no matter what, and if I had to suffer the same fate, so be it. I didn't want to leave Penelope, but protecting her was more important than my immortality. My princess had been born to save the world from vampirism. I had been born to get her there.

"I have some blood I stole from that demon we turned. We need to drink it before we go," Ian said. "It tastes like black licorice, but it'll make us alert and prepared for anything. I noticed it'd increased my senses." He rubbed his ear, cocking his head to the side.

"I've got pixie dust. Just a few lines will increase our strength enough to snap a neck as easily as Penelope did tonight. It's not the shitty kind either—top-shelf, black market. Zero high, all rapid ability." Drake arched an eyebrow.

"Whatever it takes," I said before leaving the room and spending my final night with Penelope.

"Did you get it settled with Finn?" Penelope asked as soon as I crept open the door.

The dim edge of sunrise streamed through the blind's slats on our window. But I didn't need light to see her. She sat up in bed, dressed in a thin-strapped satin gown. Her pale skin gleamed like moonlight, illuminating the dark bed in a warm, inviting glow. The memory of her bruising kiss when I'd rescued her from Priscilla's flooded my thoughts.

She'd been so helpless as a human. I never told her, but

the life had left her eyes the moment her godmother died. The only flicker of her past self had come when she opened them the first time as a vampire. Whatever untapped energy she possessed now abundantly snaked through her.

"You're supposed to be asleep," I said, hoping the edge in my voice didn't betray my agitation.

She snorted, falling back on the bed and throwing an arm over her eyes. "I don't sleep. Not with a million things on my mind. I didn't even get to go over proper dinner etiquette with Garona. What if they expect her to sit down and eat with them?"

I inched forward, stripping my clothes and leaving them lying in a messy path toward the bed. "There's no time for that, I'm afraid. The meeting is tomorrow night." I slid in bed next to her, resting my chin on a palm and studying her reaction.

She flung her arm to her side and bolted upright. Her hair flowed down her shoulders like water, disappearing into the dip of her lower back and bringing my senses to life.

"No. It's entirely too soon. No one's prepared," she responded in a sharp tone.

"We're never prepared, so let's make the best of it."

I tossed the blankets aside, revealing her slender thighs before pulling her back down to me. A sense of urgency raged through me as I climbed on top of her, slipping my fingers underneath her shoulder straps and easing them down with a quick jerk. Her nipples instantly firmed as I ripped the gown off of her, splitting it at the seams.

She gasped, rising to meet me with an angry, punishing kiss, leaving my mouth burning with raw desire. A faint taste of sunlight tingled against my tongue. Passion overtook me, growing as strong as the ache to feed. Except I couldn't feed on her anymore. Not tonight.

I tore myself away from her and growled. My fangs hung low, brushing my lower lip with needlelike pricks.

"I want this to mean something. I'm having a hard time controlling myself. I wanted to take it slow tonight." I slid my hand across her silken belly before exploring her thighs. But there was no disguising my body's reaction to her. My cock grew thick, pressing firm against her leg with a dizzying need.

Her brow creased as she trailed her hands up my arms and over my back, slowly raking her nails down my skin. The cool touch of her palms sent a chill up my spine.

"It always means something. I don't want it slow. Take me tonight like there might not be a tomorrow." She teased her legs further apart, arching her body toward me and hanging on.

I closed my eyes and swallowed hard, powerless to resist her pleas.

My hard body raked against her breasts as I slid down between her legs, feathering my tongue in a savage intensity against her clit. I ran my fingers up her slit, spreading her so that I could lap her up with each rough stroke of my tongue. She bucked against my mouth, pressing the back of my head firmly into her while she rode my face.

I pushed myself up and sat on my knees in front of her, unable to hold out any longer. I flicked the tip of my dick across her clit, soaking myself in her wetness before diving inside. The shock of her velvet pussy clenching my cock scorched through me in a heat wave I'd not felt since she turned. A weak pulse throbbed inside my chest. She bared her fangs beneath her quivering lips.

I reached for her wrists and pinned them over her head before burying myself into her further. She moaned, wrapping her legs around my waist and clutching me with a painful force. I grew tight with strain, holding her viciousness back in a playful balance of pain and pleasure. But she fought me off in one turbulent move, breaking free from my grasp. She threw me off of her and onto my back, climbing atop my dick before I realized what had just happened.

"That's quite the trick," I exhaled as she brought us back to a rhythmic tempo of filthy lust.

Her breasts bounced with each thrust as she pumped her pussy up and down my shaft. She reached around her back, stroking my balls and coaxing my pleasure right out of me. Her hips circled on my lap, sending a tingle down to the tip of my toes. A rush of need rippled through me like lightning as I buckled underneath her.

"I have to bite. I feel it. I. Can't. Stop." She leaned forward, fanning her fingers over my chest in an iron grip and forcing her lips apart in a devilish grin.

In one quick swoop, she swept down and nuzzled her nose against my collar, sinking her fangs deep into my neck. Her moans came in waves as she pushed herself against me over and over again with each gulp of blood. Her pussy pulsed in rhythm with the faint heartbeat I'd felt fading from my veins. Each suck of her mouth brought me to the tide of release until I spilled out inside of her.

She slowed her pace before coming to a complete stop.

"I'm so sorry! I don't know what overcame me. I've never needed to do that!" She pulled away from me, wiping her lips across the back of her hand.

"It's natural. Well, for vampires."

"Yeah, but … I'm not that vampy! Besides, we've never tested what your blood might do to me. What if it kills me?" She brought her hand to her chest in a dramatic move I remembered from long ago when she had been just a mere princess.

"You're already dead."

"You know what I mean!" She rolled off of me and propped herself up onto her elbow beside me.

"Do you feel any different?" I asked.

"No."

"Well then, I'd say, you're okay. Besides, my blood isn't special like yours. The most you'll get out of me is maybe a taste for you. But that would be weird."

"I've experienced weirder." She laughed, giving me a quick peck. Her lips were still moist with my blood.

"You can say that again." I rubbed my wound and smiled. I'd never been bitten by a vampire before.

My urge to bite into the dead was nonexistent. But with Penelope's mysteries, I'd prepared myself for anything.

"Just so you know, there's this place I like. It's right here." She brushed her fingertips along my collar and down to the space between my neck and shoulder. "There's nowhere I'd rather be than right there. When you're on top of me, I pull you into me, close my eyes, nuzzle into that spot, and the world disappears. All I see is your skin, slick against mine. All I feel is your body moving in rhythm with mine, covering me and keeping me safe. And all I hear are the soft moans escaping both of our lips, like we're summoning some euphoric, drugging feeling that only exists for you and me. That's our spell. We make it. At that moment, all I have is you, and all you have is me. There's no bullshit, drama, or goats. Just love."

I tucked my arm under her head and pulled her down to me. She fell, weightless, in my arms.

"Wow. You need to drink from me more often." I pressed my lips to the tip of her head.

She playfully bopped me on the nose and laughed.

"I'm serious. It's not your blood. This is just how I feel. You're my personal security blanket. I lose my worries, my stresses, and my thoughts when I'm nestled right here." She dug her cheek further into the nook of my shoulder. "I would give up everything if it meant I could stay next to you like this forever."

"You have a spot I like too," I said, whispering into her hairline.

She intertwined her legs with mine and leaned back, catching my eye. "Oh yeah? Let me guess." She reached for my hand, dragging it down between her legs. "Is that the spot you like?"

"Well, yes. But … I was trying to be Prince Charming."

"Oh. Okay. Go on." She dropped my hand, flashing a devilish look across her gaze.

"It's here." I pointed to the spot between her breasts, where her heartbeat had once lulled me into a trancelike peace.

"But there's nothing there anymore."

"There doesn't have to be. I'll never forget the way your heartbeat felt, pulsing through my veins. Even without a heart, you still fill me with sunshine," I spoke with gentle softness, reassuring her of how much she meant to me.

"Really?"

"Without a doubt. I'm starting to think the whole heart-less-vampire thing is just a theory. Just because we can't see it doesn't mean it's not still there. Kind of like a soul. We believe in those, yet we can't see our souls. Our hearts are the same. They didn't disappear. They only went into hiding. I don't need a pulse to tell me I'm alive. I feel alive when I'm with you, heartless or not."

"So, you still feel love? Affection? Emotions? Even when you're not drinking from me? Even when I'm dead?"

"Especially when you're dead. You're worth more than your miraculous blood, Penelope. It wasn't just your blood that did this to me. It's you."

She dipped her head and sniffled. "Promise you'll come back to me?" she asked.

"I promise."

"After tomorrow, I was thinking of asking Mirror Mirror to find Fritzi. Maybe it'll be safe for her to come here with The Council gone. I'm sure she would donate blood for more trials. We can work with my old blood, too, so we can try to start a family or turn back and live a quiet life—or both. I'm ready."

My mood spiraled at the mention of her blood. I started to tell her about the dwindling supply, but the words hitched in my throat. I thought better than to force them out. The risk of running out of the cure gnawed away at my confidence for a future, but I tucked the thought away as soon as it formed. The last thing I wanted to do was leave Penelope with worry. She needed to trust that I had this under control. After all, I had been Prince Charming at one point in my life. Saving the princess had always been in my blood.

"Sounds like a perfect plan," I said without hesitation.

"Good. I can't wait for our happily ever after."

"Me neither." I pulled her into a tighter embrace.

A newly awakened sense of life, even after death, comforted me. Her hopes had unlocked a heart I didn't have.

FROM THE DESK OF FRITZI COX

Dear Reader,

The knowledge I've gained after my meeting with Loure Ankerton is mind-blowing. When I set out for my trip to the mental ward, I brought along my husband, Henry, and a digital recorder to make sure I could transcribe the details of our conversation to you with one hundred percent accuracy. My noted experience and conversations are entirely true. The only time I did not document our meeting was when Loure asked me to turn the recorder off and asked about Priscilla. I recounted what little I knew of her death and probed for answers about her involvement with the vampires and her old apothecary business with Gertie.

But Loure stayed silent for a long while before agreeing to share his late wife's story. He said that he felt like he could redeem her in my eyes and maybe offer me another point of view for the mistakes she'd made. I did not let on that I knew very little about the witch's life and death. The small amount of news I'd received about Morningwood Manor crumbling was from a short article in Abe's bookshop and my own minimal research. I wanted Priscilla's life story straight from the source. So, naturally, I let my interviewee do the talking, only interrupting during minor details I wanted him to expand on.

After our conversation, I immediately felt sick. I could never forgive Priscilla for the cruel things she had done. But now, I have a better grasp of the depth of her traumatized character. If you're interested in reading about Priscilla's life, you can find that story in Home Sweet Home. But please be forewarned: it is not for the faint of heart. Her tale is dark, and once you choose to read it, you can't unsee it. You'll be haunted by her grave decisions and tortured soul forever. After learning what I know now, without a doubt, I'll never be the same. Tread lightly.

The following conversation is repeated verbatim. All details are valid. Nothing has been embellished.

My husband and I arrived at Forks University's mental health ward at approximately three o'clock p.m. on a Tuesday. We were greeted by Sheila, the head nurse I'd spoken with on the phone. She asked about our connection with John Doe, and my clever husband filled in all the gaps with a made-up story of adoption while I took a deeper look at my surroundings. I had to admit that I paid no attention to Henry's lies. I trusted him to take care of all the technicalities of getting us into this place, allowing me to free mental space and energy to do my job as a reporter and investigate. He never let me down.

The residents had just finished snack time, which consisted of milk and cookies in a small break room that smelled of mothballs and dried-out Play-Doh. Coloring books lay strewn atop the tables, the thin carpet was stained every color imaginable, and in the corner of the room, an antique television sat atop a three-legged stand. The wooden top looked as if someone had chewed it. The irony that this place of death was much like a place of beginning was not lost on me. The ward was a preschool for the dying.

On the TV screen, a pair of worn sock puppets performed a comedic skit. I recognized the show as the same one that kept my daughter's attention when I turned our television on so that I could get a bit of work done. But there wasn't any entertainment here. The puppets were performing for a nearly dead room.

Four residents were gathered around the television, all in low-slung wheelchairs. Two slept, hunched over in positions that made my body ache, just looking at them. Their heads were bent at odd angles, exposing the brittle bones protruding through the thin skin on the back of their necks. Their spines looked as if they could snap in half under the gentlest touch. The other two residents looked toward the TV screen, staring past it without blinking. The vacancy in their eyes hovered in between an existence I couldn't understand. They did not laugh at the puppets' jokes.

"Right this way, Ms. Vanderbilt." The nurse tore my attention from the break room and motioned for me to follow.

I snapped my eyes to Henry, who winked before scurrying behind me on my heels. We walked down a narrow hall, our footsteps rudely echoing off the bare walls and signaling our arrival. Passing each open door, we saw a resident lying in a hospital bed, staring at the ceiling. Some would turn their head and watch us pass. Others didn't bother.

"Do you get many visitors here, Sheila?" I asked, recoiling at a splattering of old, muddied blood against white tile.

"You're the first visitor here in the last several months," she said. "Most of my patients' families have long since forgotten about them. They don't care to visit people who don't remember them anyway. *What's the point?* That's the excuse they tell me. But really, they just don't want to know. Once you set foot into this reality, you can't go back. No one wants this sad existence in their heads." She stopped in front of the last door on the left.

Somewhere in the distance, a woman screamed, followed by a jarring alarm, rhythmically repeating a 525 code. A team of nurses emerged from doorways, rushing toward a room just outside of my view. They stampeded across the ward in a blend of pastel scrubs and rubber sneakers squeaking across the floor. The exit lights blinked overhead. Sheila took off down the hallway in a run.

"Maybe we should go back." I turned to my husband, who stepped in front of me, blocking my view down the hall.

He pointed at the scribbled whiteboard sign on the door next to us. It read, *John Doe.*

"We're here. Better do this now while they're distracted. I think Sheila was onto me. Let's go." He grabbed my hand and pushed open the door.

The walls inside were painted a dingy, washed-out salmon and covered with marks. In the corner of the room, Loure sat upright in a hospital bed. His hands lay clasped atop his lap. The skin across his knuckles stretched like aged crepe paper.

"They did that for you, you know." His thin lips parted in a smile, displaying a row of ocher-stained teeth.

"Who did what?" I asked, pausing just inside the doorway.

Henry clicked the door shut behind him.

"The pixies. They distracted Sheila and her gang, so you could come here and tell me how you killed my wife. I know she's dead. I felt it all the way over here from the other side. Heartbreak travels both realms."

"There's been some kind of mistake. I didn't kill your wife. I haven't seen any pixies either." I inched forward.

The room smelled like a mixture of wet dogs and cigarettes.

Henry nudged my side and tilted his head toward a cracked window. Grass clippings and petals were scattered across the sill, leading to an empty bird's nest on a nearby shelf.

"They're not in there. I told you, they're distracting the nurses, so you can tell me about my wife. You wouldn't see my pixie friends anyway. You can't. You don't have The Crux —just me. But something tells me you know more than most humans. Tell me, did it get loose?"

"I don't know what you mean by that. But I don't know much. It's why I'm here. I'd like to understand better. I'm a reporter. My husband … he was once a genie."

"Aha! I knew there was more than meets the eye with you two." He let out a long sigh. "I just want you to know that I don't blame you for offing her. She had it coming for a long time."

"But we didn't. We can't even return to that realm if we wanted to."

His bloodshot eyes sank deep into the hollows of his skull.

"Well then, who did?" he asked, studying my reaction.

"I'm not entirely sure, but I think it might have something to do with The Council, sir," I said in a low, composed voice, hoping I wouldn't betray my uselessness.

After all, I wanted information from Loure in exchange for nothing. Until I was able to speak directly with Penelope, I was borderline clueless about recent events in Morningwood. I'd purposely stayed away for the safety of my family.

"Of course it does. Of course. Then, why are you here?" His tone reflected a guilty bitterness.

"You mentioned The Crux. I'm assuming that's the realm-straddling disease. I'd like to know more about it, so we can return to the fantastical dimension." I pressed my lips together, mentally measuring the line between saying too much and too little.

"You don't want to straddle realms as a human. Everyone will think you're insane. I've lived here for decades, wasting away." His eyes briefly brimmed over with tears before he blinked them back and looked away.

"Can't you just return to Morningwood if you straddle realms?" Henry asked.

"Do you know what the word *crux* means?" Loure ignored my husband and focused his gaze on me.

"It's like a problem," I answered.

"Correct. The point at which one has to solve a nearly impossible problem. Kind of like you're stuck at a crossroads. That's what happens when you contract this disease. You're stuck."

"I don't understand." I shifted my weight on my feet. "But can I record this, please? I'd like to be able to go back and listen for anything I might miss. It sounds fascinating."

I pulled a recorder from my purse and waited. Loure nodded, giving me his permission.

"Might as well. I estimate I only have days left in me anyway. Someone's got to carry on my research."

I clicked the record button and held it between us, wary of getting too close to the diseased man.

He slumped forward and began. "When a vampire bites a human or creature, the victim's body reacts to the poison, painfully turning him. There's a very, very brief moment that his DNA pauses its restructuring and meets at a crossroads. It can stand strong enough to become unaffected; it can completely combust, and the victim could die; or it could continue restructuring into its final vampire form. It's a chemical reaction at a cellular level. Almost ninety-eight percent of the time, The Crux turns and chooses the path of the vampire. But some of those patients get stuck in that DNA re-sequencing. Their bodies and minds are caught in between worlds. They fade in and out. That's why it's also known as The Fade. This suspension between worlds means they're losing their minds."

"The Fade?" Henry stumbled back into the wall. A tremble crept along the edge of his jaw until he cleared his throat and regained his composure.

I'd never seen my husband terrified of anything.

"The Fade," Loure repeated in a firm and final tone, looking at us both.

"I've never heard of it. Is it centralized to humans after they're bitten? How can that be if you had it there, and now, you're here, straddling both worlds? What made you fade without completely losing your mind?" I shuffled nearer to his bed, holding the recorder closer to him.

"It's not a strain specific to anyone. It attacks everyone, magic or not. It originated in vampires, but it mutated throughout the supernatural dimension. It affects every creature differently. But for the most part, vampires seem to bear the brunt of it ... and humans. Vampires already straddle realms, so it doesn't cause any change there. But it puts their bodies and minds in a state of constant conflict. This usually drives the patients mad enough to withdraw or harm themselves. They don't always fade from existence. Some vampires who've had it still see the fantastical in a blur, as if they were looking through a magic mirror. But most of the time, they choose to end their existence. The torture is unbearable. I'm only here because my attacker gratefully chose to inject me with the smallest of drops. I think a splash in my evening wine did it."

"Who was your attacker?" I asked.

"My wife, Priscilla. Whether or not she wanted to do that to torture me, I never got to ask."

A bead of sweat formed at my brow as I looked from my husband to Loure and back again. Henry's face had turned pale and was pinched with the discovery of whatever The Fade meant to him. By the sheer look of terror on his face, I felt that my reckless concern was justified, and my next move wouldn't be up to debate.

"If you have it, are you still contagious?" Henry asked.

"No. Not at my level. At least, I don't think so. I spent years studying this disease. I know the scary rumors make it seem like anyone can contract the disease, but that's simply not true. It's extremely rare to contract without being directly injected because it's a naturally occurring disease inside the body, much like cancer. We nearly had it eradicated from Morningwood altogether, and to my knowledge, it still is. There was only one sample of it left. If I know my late wife, she had it locked away for safekeeping for her own selfish reasons. At least, until she decided she needed to bring it out again. I wonder if that had anything to do with her death." He scratched a balding patch of silver hair atop his head. A scaly layer of skin covered his scalp with blood-speckled age spots.

"So, let me get this straight. You studied The Crux and managed to contain it. Then, Priscilla vanished you and your own work, sending you spiraling into a maddening state of mental illness for … reasons. But now, she's dead, so someone has the sample. Right?" I rubbed the bridge of my nose with my free hand and squinted.

"If I were to guess, I would say The Council got ahold of it from her," he said, shrugging with defeat.

I swallowed hard with the realization that my urgent travel to Bostwick might not come quick enough.

"Those bastards enslaved me as part of their research for years. They wanted to use it as a biological weapon. I tried to blow them off as much as I could and focus my time and energy on Priscilla and Gertie's apothecary. But the leaders of The Council always came sniffing at our door, asking for updates on my research." Loure spat out the words in a low, tormented voice.

"I'd tinkered with the disease enough to know that it was easily, manually mutated in the lab. And if some of those mutations got out and into the hands of the wrong people, our entire world as we knew it could end. I put powerful abilities, unique to every creature imaginable, in some of those trials. Priscilla and Gertie knew this too. They even hid some of the DNA into seeds they planted for their business in hopes that The Council wouldn't ever find them. What good is a bunch of seeds to vampires? My wife and her friend sold youth creams, not deadly weapons. At least, that was what most people thought." A sparkle flashed across his face before disappearing into the same glassy-eyed expression he'd worn since we'd arrived.

"Penelope," Henry whispered, stepping up next to me.

I met his gaze and shook my head, signaling for him not to mention anything further. If Penelope was a deadly weapon to both of our worlds, no one could know about it. But the thought raised more questions than we had time to ask. I had to warn the princess before The Council unleashed The Crux.

"Why would The Council risk messing with The Crux if it could make them human again? They don't want that. Couldn't it essentially act as a cure then?" I switched the recorder in my palms.

"Oh, it's nothing like a cure. Sure, it can revert them back to their human form. But like I said, it wouldn't be the same human form they knew. It's as much torture for a vampire or any magical creature as it is on a human. Maybe even more so. The Council wants to collect that power and use it to banish their enemies. Easier than killing them, I suppose.

"The only reason I'm here and able to talk about it is because I've studied it. When Priscilla injected me, she had the decency for once in her life to add only a drop to my wine instead of stabbing me in the heart. A full dose, and I would have not only vanished completely, but I'd also never remember who I was or where I came from. I would just know I didn't belong here. But I remember everything. She spared me the torture of losing myself."

"Why would she do such a thing?" Henry asked. The corners of his lips turned up in disgust.

"You know she's Grundle's daughter, right?" Loure asked.

"Grundle? The witch named after the spot between a man's ass and balls? That Grundle? The one who lived in the gingerbread house? She's not real. That's just a fairy tale. Now, you're just messing with us." Henry folded his arms over his chest and blew out a breath.

"It's true. She's the witch with the unfortunate name. That was Priscilla's mother. She grew up in that gingerbread house. To my knowledge, it's still there. Though Priscilla tore down the sugared walls and rebuilt it as just a plain old cottage. It's hidden deep in the forest, near Bostwick Winery. But I wouldn't go looking for it. That area's ripe with curses. It's rumored that the soil's contaminated from …" His voice trailed off into a strained silence.

"The blood of Grundle's victims. The children she lured into her gingerbread house." Henry's voice fell flat.

"Oh my." I put a hand to my throat and held back a wave of nausea.

Priscilla's crumbling shack Penelope had escaped to was really a graveyard. I wondered if Gertie's plan all along had been to destroy the cursed cottage while saving her princess.

"My wife had a troubled upbringing. I'll talk no more about it unless that recorder is off. I'd like to do her story justice. But I don't want to go on record with it. You can say

74

I'm at a crux with the way I feel about her. I hate her, yet I don't," Loure said, rubbing his bare ring finger.

"I'm really sorry about her death," I lied.

He broke into a leisurely smile, edged with a touch of manic.

"Don't be. She was wicked," he said as his eyes grew an inky black, dilating with anticipation.

I clicked the recorder off.

By the time Loure finished his story, he lay, winded and dozing in and out of a feverish dream. I stood, turning the recorder in my hand and organizing my thoughts.

"I know what you're thinking. I think you'd better speak with that Finn guy. He seems to know all about the lab stuff. I bet if he can get ahold of that sample, he can alter it just enough for us to straddle realms without turning batshit crazy." Henry pressed his palm to my lower back. His touch still sent a spark along my spine, even after all this time.

"Us?" I asked, searching his eyes for answers.

"You think you're going to the other side without me?"

"What about Elly?"

"What about Elly? We aren't leaving her. We'll still be the same. The only thing that will change is, you'll be able to talk to the creatures in that realm yourself, and I can go with you to protect you. Our home is still here, in the human world. But I understand your need to return and investigate. I won't let you travel that road alone. We both do it or not at all." He drew himself up to his full height, reminding me of the genie I'd once known.

"Fine. Let me talk to Penelope. We have to warn her anyway before The Council unleashes this shit in Morning-wood. The brothers will have to stop them."

Loure rolled over and let out a thundering snore.

"We aren't even sure if it's The Council who has that last sample. Do you really want to go to Bostwick, a place teeming with vamps? Can't you just call her up?" Henry whispered.

"I tried weeks ago, and she hung up on me. We have to go —and fast. They need to know about The Crux before they're infected." I stashed the recorder in my purse and exited through the door, pulling my husband along behind me.

"You're going to play her the recording?" His voice came out in a high-pitched squeal.

"No. I'm destroying that—after I write my piece. But I'll leave it for the reader to decide if they want to go down that path—viewer discretion advised. I won't pull a Grundle and sugarcoat it, but some of those events Loure described should stay buried at the cottage. There's no sense in me repeating what we've learned and releasing such evil out into the world."

Reader, I have gone back and edited the story for accuracy where I needed to include the things I'd learned—most notably, Garona's story. As morbid as this will read, I'm documenting my knowledge from the moment I learn of it in case I'm demolished by a vampire or infected with a deadly disease and cursed into internal madness.

My husband is by my side, and my daughter is safe and secure at a top-secret location. We are taking all precautions and have it under good authority that we will win this war. The fight has just begun, but our tenacity grows, unfaded.

CHAPTER FIVE

PENELOPE

I SPENT THE HOURS BEFORE GARONA'S DEPARTURE TEACHING her the bare essentials for her big event. Just a few short months ago, I'd stood in this same ballroom, practicing for my performance. That little adventure had turned out to be quite the disaster. I prayed my clone wouldn't suffer the same sickening fate even if her circuits were so crossed that she didn't understand a single thing other than basic commands. At least, that was what Finn had told me. But the spark in her eye wasn't just from blowing a fuse in her wired brain. I sensed some form of spirit lurking beneath her surface. Whether it was a lively charm or an intelligent code, she was more than just a robotic doppelgänger.

"From the top now. Show me how you walk into the room and seat yourself. Pretend Vail is sitting on the right." I tipped my head to the corner seat of a long table I'd set up for this exact lesson.

Trevor sat in one of the folding chairs, yawning and flicking his tail back and forth, seemingly bored with our shenanigans. Otto lay across the table like a Christmas ham. And Grump ... Grump had passed out under the table after his second bucket of wine. After our test in manners, he'd given us a solid score of nine out of ten and blacked out.

Garona gathered her dress in her hands, subtly lifting it to reveal a pair of unbreakable charmed glass slippers. The last pair she'd worn shattered under her lumbering ogre stomps. But I'd quickly nipped that unattractive behavior in the bud and taught her how to glide across the floor like a true princess in much sturdier footwear. She sashayed past me with a breathtaking smile, rendering me speechless for once. I tugged at my collar and gulped. All of the princessy qualities I'd lost had found their way into my boneheaded clone. She tucked her dress underneath her bottom and regally sat upright in her chair.

"Beautiful. Well done!" I clapped my hands together.

Otto rolled over onto his swollen belly and began to snore.

My family hadn't yet grown used to my new waking hours. Only Garona could survive without rest.

"Okay, now, come here, and let's work on a little dance. Just in case they make you perform. Predators like to play with their prey. I wouldn't put it past those bastards to force you to entertain them and have a little fun at your expense. I doubt things will get that far though. They'll be—" I drew my finger across my neck and stuck my tongue out of the corner of my mouth, gagging.

She mimicked my gesture and nodded.

"Ten! Ten!" she repeated the words she'd learned from Grump.

Her head bobbled atop her neck, squeaking like a busted bedspring. I made a mental note to make sure Finn tightened her screws or oiled her rigs—or whatever the hell one did to make a clone more human. The only trait remotely human about my twin—besides her sudden onset of fear—was the perfectly accurate skin suit she wore to cover whatever workings she hid underneath. I never asked Finn exactly what he'd stuffed inside of her. I didn't want to know.

I thought she could handle human life, just as I had. After all, I'd watched her chug an entire bottle of wine. But the one time I had tried to treat Garona like a human and feed her magic bean water, she'd sprung a leak out of her belly button and short-circuited, collapsing to the floor in the same way I did when I poured one glass of wine too many. Grump had scored her and followed suit. Our tipsy flaw ran in the family.

I dug my heels into the ground and lifted my hands, levitating chairs and tables out of the way to clear the dance floor. Trevor hopped down from his comfortable spot and scurried toward the edge of the room. Otto lazily curled his body and somersaulted across the ballroom, barreling into his fox friend like a bowling ball. Grump still snoozed in a deep slumber. I levitated him out of the way, resting his body atop a stack of empty oak barrels in the corner.

The oversize crystal chandelier that I'd once hung on to so that I could make a dramatic entrance no longer existed. The night of the massacre, it had shattered to pieces, taking my light with it. The brothers had replaced it with basic hanging fixtures situated in several rows across the ceiling, but the ballroom had already lost its appeal. I paused, allowing myself to reminisce about how important royal balls and castles used to be to me.

As an innocent princess, I'd spent my days dreaming of golden chariots, self-sweeping brooms dragging across my castle floor, and diamond rings big enough to catch the sunlight and burn a hole through a silken blouse. But as a vampire princess, my dreams had turned to nightmares, and my power had become unyielding. I gave a long, dramatic sigh and tucked my problems away. I'd find the right balance one day—after I disposed of my enemies. My only problem was, I kept gaining more and more of them.

"Aha! You must be about to dance. You know, it's been a long time since I've watched you work the room. I can't wait to see this," Vail called behind me, pulling up a chair and swirling it around.

He climbed on top, straddling it backward and resting his forearms across the back. His boyish excitement sent a wave of heat through my thighs, buckling them in place.

"Aren't you supposed to be bottling up my blood in fancy, new packaging?" I asked.

"Done and done. We couldn't exactly call it Royal Blend, like you suggested. We're saving that branding later for the miserable vampires who can make use of it. We labeled the batch we're serving tonight Moondust, at Ian's assistance. He has a background in moonshine. It's a passion of his, I suppose. Anyway, Moondust is a combination of fairy dust and grapes, harvested in the moonlight. That's why it sparkles. At least, that is what they'll think. It's really your golden blood hidden in there, ready to poison them so I can murder their human bodies in cold blood. Cold, vampy blood. I can promise you that." He shrugged, as if the vow he'd repeated was just another mundane task.

Garona swooned on her feet, watching the exchange between Vail and me.

"I was going to teach her how to dance. Just in case they ask for entertainment. I know men. At the royal balls back in Poppycock, the court always asked for a quick twirl whenever Theo hosted a gathering. Of course, I happily obliged, lifting my skirt to reveal a swarm of butterflies and bunnies. Everyone loved that trick. But with Garona … eh, I don't want to know what Finn sewed together under her skirt. I'm just going to have to make do with what I got and show her how to skip to a beat or something. I haven't quite figured it out." I tapped my finger to my chin.

Garona never took her eyes off of Vail.

"Let me help you." He swung his leg around the chair and stood up, adjusting his cuff links.

He was already dressed for his business meeting in a navy-blue tailored suit. His thick, wavy hair was combed back and set as if he'd placed each strand perfectly in its correct position. I had the sudden urge to pounce on him from behind and drink from his collar again but quieted my fragile resistance. He had tasted of raw, feral desire with a faint hint of danger, and I couldn't get enough.

"May I have this dance, please, madam?" He sauntered toward Garona, bowing and extending a hand.

She looked up at him and smiled, stupefied at the magnificent man smiling back at her. I knew it wasn't the half-ogre brain causing her goofy grin because I wore the same expression each time he shot me his pearly-white fangs. Vail could mesmerize me to do anything he wanted without using his hypnotizing vampy abilities. One look at my man, and I very clearly remembered the heartbeat I'd once had. My fangs hung low in my mouth, salivating for a scandalous act we didn't have time for.

He cleared his throat, returning my attention to the task at hand. "Can you summon some music? Is that even possible? Our sound system still doesn't work. But I think we need something to practice to. I could hum, but—"

"Say no more." I waved him away.

I'd secretly practiced this summons in the shower when he wasn't around. I'd stumbled upon my new power by accident when I tried to sing some of the old lullabies Gertie had taught me. But as soon as I opened my mouth, I became a real-life one-man—*ahem*—woman band.

I took a deep breath and conjured the image of a royal

orchestra in my mind. The rumble started in my bosom, escaping through my parted lips in waves. The soft, melodic beat of brass and strings drifted out of my mouth, acting as a loudspeaker.

Vail's jaw dropped, but I shook my head, not wanting to break my trance. I knew I looked like a fool, but my nitwit clone looked even worse. She began to drool as he took her hand and pulled her across the room. Her distracted steps refused to match his. Instead, she fell into his chest any chance she could get and began to hump his leg like a wolf in heat. He propped her back up, swaying to the beat, but again and again, she kept returning to his leg. I didn't know which was the worst spectacle—her or me.

I cringed, ashamed of myself for displaying a part of my DNA sequence in Garona that reflected my personality at one hundred percent accuracy. Finn had nailed my unlady-like voraciousness for sexy men on the head, but I didn't want Vail to know that. I still had to keep somewhat of a princess appearance. True to his gentleman nature, Vail ignored Garona's advances and kept twirling her around the room, keeping her at arm's length with his brute strength. But when the melody slowed, escaping my lips in a sputter-ing-out hiss, he quickly stopped, backing away from her.

"I think I hear Ian calling. I have to finish packing the car. I'll see you two in a bit!" He ran off faster than I could shut my mouth and tune myself out.

I glanced at Garona, who stood with a smile stretched so wide across her face that I saw the corner of her mouth begin to crack.

"Let's take a breath and focus on not doing that. Ever. If The Council asks you to dance, break your leg off or some-thing. Just snap it in half. Whatever you do, don't make that little move, or we're busted."

I pinched the bridge of my nose and thinned my lips. It

didn't matter if I was princess me, vampire me, or clone me; I'd proven to be a lost cause in any form.

WINTER'S last chill left as quickly as it had come. Any evidence of snow had melted, leaving the ground slick with a muddy sludge. I stood outside the winery, avoiding puddles and watching as the brothers packed their car with weapons and gadgets I hadn't known they possessed. Two shotguns, three pistols, a pile of stakes, and four cans of whoop-ass later, they declared themselves prepared.

"Why do you need all that? Can't you just rip their heads from their spines? Do any of you even know how to shoot a gun?" I folded my arms.

Beside me, Garona stuck out her hip and mimicked my gesture.

Ian swiftly drew a pistol from beneath his jacket and shot a round of bullets at the old scarecrow looming in the vineyard. The scarecrow snapped, falling into a pile of rotting pumpkins beneath him—remnants from the investor ball. I doubted we would ever host such an extravagant event again. After the massacre, our lively winery had been reduced to a cursed graveyard.

"Impressive." I smirked.

He blew the tip of his pistol and stuffed it back into the holster. Finn stood at a distance, observing the spectacle with an air of bitterness. He'd, for once, wanted to leave his laboratory, but his role as my bodyguard wasn't optional. Vail had made sure he understood that.

"Don't you know Ian used to be a cowboy? He was some type of champion dueler way out west. Someplace called Gillibrook. Isn't that right, Ian?" Vail appeared from behind me with a case of Moondust. He walked it over to the trunk of the car and nestled it inside.

"Yep. That was my hometown. I spent my days riding horses and my nights staring up at the moon." A far-off look clouded Ian's face before he disappeared into the backseat.

"Ma-ma." Garona pointed to the sky.

A deep ache sent a shock wave through my chest.

"Yes. She's watching over you tonight. You're going to do great. Remember to showcase your best princessy qualities. Twirls, curtsies, smiles. Okay?" I curled my palms over her shoulders and turned her toward me.

She stared down at her feet, avoiding my gaze.

"Uh-uh-uh." I tipped her chin up with my finger. "Don't look down. Always keep your chin up. You've got this. Just let the brothers do their business and don't speak. I'll see you right after they're done." The words grew thick in my throat. I was sending my clone into a battle she knew nothing about.

"Prom-hiss?" She balled her dress in her hands, clutching and twisting the material into a wrinkled mess.

I didn't bother to correct her.

Vail shut the trunk and walked back to us. A heavy, stifled tension filled the air, pulling me to him like a magnet. My lips tingled in remembrance of his touch the night before.

"I promise. Vail will keep you safe." I let my hands fall to my sides and stepped back, holding a breath I didn't need.

Garona turned to leave, walking a slow death march to the car.

"We're going to be late. Let's go!" Drake called from the driver's seat. He flicked on the headlights, illuminating a warm glow on the misty road ahead.

The chorus of crickets and frogs echoing through the nearby woods stopped. A warning whispered in my head.

"What if I stay in the car? You can signal if you need me.

I'd feel much better there with you. I don't want you to go alone, Vail. What if—" I started.

He put his hands up, stopping me. I gritted my teeth and held the screams of frustration at the back of my throat.

"We've been through this. I can't lose you again," he said.

"Oh yeah? And what if I lose you this time? Think I can handle that?"

We stood, staring at each other, stubbornly silent.

The sound of a zipper ripped through the night, drawing our attention back to the awaiting car. Finn tossed a bag inside and waved his brothers good-bye.

"As soon as I get back, we're done with shit like this. No more death, or fear, or tragedy. No more vengeance and bitchcraft or lies and curses. After I'm home, it's just me and you and a future full of possibilities. I want rainbows and sunshine again. Hell, give me a sprinkle of pink glitter over this grim reality any day. I'll gladly dance with the demons if it means I get to come back to you. You're what I've been searching for. You're my sunshine. Think I'm going to let you go that easy?" He blew out a breath. "These fuckers won't know what hit them."

I threw my arms around his neck and nuzzled into his nook.

"I believe in you," I said, swallowing a burning lump in my throat. "For the cause."

"For us." He took a step back, grabbing my hand and bowing before brushing his lips across my knuckles. His fangs nipped my fingers.

"I love you," I whispered, closing my eyes and fighting back a rush of tears.

"I love you too."

When I opened my eyes, he was gone.

I couldn't tear my gaze from the taillights as the car rumbled down the driveway. I stood, patiently watching until the thick fog rolling ahead swallowed their car, making it vanish from my view. My senses awakened to high alert. Rows of glowing eyes dotted through the forest, waking at their departure. A wolf howled in the distance. The scent of a skunk drifted through the air.

"Come on. Let's go inside," Finn called from behind me.

I blinked, peering into the dark and listening for any threats, but the night was as dead as I was. Any hint of life stopped at the winery's gates.

I turned to go, following behind him and pausing to examine a dead bird lying on the pavement.

"Finn, stop. Wait! What's this?" I knelt, cradling the blue-bird in my palm. Its wings stuck out at an odd angle.

"It probably flew into the window." He hovered above me, sticking his nose into the air and sniffing. "Do you smell cigar smoke?"

"Faintly. Maybe it's this poor little guy. Maybe he had a long night out and overdid it on the partying." I stood up, bringing the bird closer to my face for inspection.

"I highly doubt your bird overdosed on cigars and … whatever you're suggesting." He sniffed the air again, prickling on high alert.

"You never know. He could have—" I began. The low buzz of an electric current ricocheted inside me, catching me off guard.

A slow, melodic whistle echoed through the trees behind us.

"Shh!" He brought a finger to his lips and jerked his head from right to left. The scent of ash and cigar grew stronger. "We need to get inside. Toss the bird. Let's go," he urged.

I drew my brows together and prepared to protest, but the bird stirred in my palms.

"Finn," I whispered, nudging his side with my elbow and bringing his attention back to me. "It's alive!"

"What? Impossible," he spoke in hushed excitement, gaping at the waking bird in my hands.

The bird rolled back and forth, stretching his fragile wings and popping them into place.

"See? I told you!"

"What did you do? How did you do that?"

"I don't know. I didn't do anything! I felt this weird electric energy inside of me when I picked it up. But I think that's just fear for Vail and them, not anything to do with this." I shoved my hands in his face.

The bird chirped before hopping to his feet, as if nothing had happened. He perched atop my fingertips and ruffled his feathers before flying away in a series of graceful twirls and swoops.

"Holy shit." He rubbed the back of his neck. "You just breathed princess energy into him. Look at him go!"

"I can use this." I stared at my hands in disbelief, turning my palms over and back. The shock of my power rendered me immobile. My feet grew heavy, firmly planting themselves into the ground.

"Let's go downstairs and figure it out. I want to show you something. I think this new skill might be able to help me with a project I've been working to create throughout my entire death." He put his hand around my arm and tugged me inside.

"And what's that?" I asked, stepping through the front door. My hands still felt heavy from the weight of whatever the hell had just happened.

"Promise not to tell my brothers?" He turned to me and caught my eye.

Mirror Mirror peered over his shoulder behind him.

"I can't make a promise if it puts us in danger."

"It doesn't. She doesn't." His eyes danced behind a veil of exhaustion.

"Okay, I promise. Go on," I said, knowing Mirror Mirror had heard every single word without swearing his silence to Finn.

"It's my fiancée. I want you to try to bring her back to life." He rubbed the back of his neck and looked away.

"What? You have a fiancée? What happened? What do you mean, bring her back?" My voice rose to a squeal.

"I have her. I ... created her. She's kind of like Garona but without the robotics. She's her. Not a clone. But her heart doesn't beat."

"You mean, she wasn't a vampire?" I detected a gut-wrenching ache as I hung on his words.

"No. She was human before, but ..." His voice faltered.

An envelope slipped under the doorstep, knocking against his worn leather shoe.

"What's this?" He picked it up and tore the envelope open, pulling out a tarot card with an arrow drawn across the top, pointing upward. The sudden excitement that had overtaken him moments ago melted from his face.

"What is it?" I grabbed the card from his hand and turned it on its back, looking for some type of explanation. "I can't read tarot cards. Is this bad?"

"They drew the arrow upright. It's the Tower, which, when upright, warns of upcoming disaster and destruction." His already-pale skin grew ghastly.

"Who the hell would put that here?"

I stomped to the door and swung it open. But only darkness and silence waited outside of the winery.

"Stop!" he yelled, barreling past me and slamming it shut before locking it. "Are you crazy?"

"No! But someone's playing games, and I'm not going to sit here and take it." I realized what was happening as soon as the words left my mouth.

Earlier, I'd warned Garona that predators liked to play

with their prey. But I wasn't someone's damn toy. I'd planned, unbeknownst to Finn's knowledge, to escape the winery and sneak into The Cave, unnoticed, as soon as he became distracted tonight, not destroy whatever evil cowardness lurked at my doorstep.

"It's The Council. They communicate through tarot. They're not playing games. They're issuing a warning. If we don't listen to it, we're ashes."

I ripped the card in half and threw it on the floor, igniting it in flames as it drifted to the ground in sparks of hot tinder.

"I'm done with games. I'm going to The Cave. Council be damned." I swerved on my heels and headed back outside.

"But, Penelope, wait!" Finn put his hand out, stopping me. His cold fingers curled around my arm, leaving white marks on my skin.

"You can't make me stay."

I sent a bolt of lightning in between us, knocking him backward off his feet. He steadied himself against the wall, pushing back up and towering over me like a spruce, rigid and prickly.

"Fuck! I wasn't going to stop you. I was going to tell you I had to get a weapon and a bottle of blood. I'm going with you."

"Why?" I asked.

"Because those bastards are why I've been carrying my fiancée's heart around in a jar for decades," he said, pulling on his collar and adjusting his lab coat.

The sound of tires squealing across the driveway stopped us both in our tracks.

"Stay back," I sneered, pushing Finn behind me.

My fingers burned at the tips. I looked around the entry, but my fox and friends were thankfully nowhere in the line of danger. The last time I'd seen them was when they slumbered in the ballroom. I took a deep breath and summoned a forceful wind to knock down whoever dared to stand on the other side. Two car doors slammed shut, followed by a rush of voices coming from the other side of the door. The hair on the back of my neck stood on end.

"Penelope! It's me, Fritzi! And Henry! Let us in, please! We need to speak with you!" Fritzi beat her fists against the door.

I let out a sigh of relief and dropped my spell. The howling wind vanished into thin air before I opened the door to find both of my friends trembling on my doorstep. A shot of panic swept through my chest as I realized that only terrible news would make them risk their human lives by visiting a deadly vampires' den.

"You're a vampire," Fritzi whispered. "I knew it."

I put my hand over my mouth, covering my fangs.

Finn stepped out from behind me, studying our guests.

Henry stiffened beside her, reaching around her back and pulling her closer to him.

Trevor, Otto, and Grump emerged from the dark, oblivious to my human friends. They circled the car, sniffing and poking at it curiously.

"I'm sorry I haven't been in touch. It's not safe here. You have to go!" I said, urging Fritzi and Henry back.

I didn't want their news. I couldn't handle their information. And the dreadful thought that whoever had planted the tarot card was probably watching us from the dark, scared me enough to shut my dear friends out of my life—death —forever.

"But you have to know! You're all in danger. I know why you vanished!" Fritzi whispered, throwing a glance over her shoulder.

"My godmother banished me. I know. She did it to save me. I've been through all of this," I said, on the brink of losing my patience.

My senses told me more than one Council member was surrounding us tonight. I heard the crack of twigs underfoot, coming from the nearby vineyards, and whoever stayed hidden in the shadows wouldn't stay there much longer once he realized we had two humans in our midst.

"No. You were flawed from the beginning. She probably only helped along the way. But what you have is The Crux," Henry spoke up, speaking to all but only looking at Finn. "The Fade."

Finn's eyes grew wide as his expression changed from curious to repulsed. He took a step back from me and ran a hand through his thick hair, disheveling it even more so than usual. "That was eradicated in our realm. It died with Loure Ankerton long ago."

"No. Loure isn't dead. We spoke with him. Priscilla had the last sample of The Crux in her possession, but we have reason to believe The Council has that now, and they're planning on unleashing it." Fritzi's words rolled off her tongue in a rush. She wrung her hands out in front of her.

"What? Why would she have that?" Finn asked.

"Priscilla and Gertie used it to alter seeds for their business. Her seed, to be exact." Fritzi lifted her chin in my direction. "Priscilla took the sample and used it to vanish her own husband. She had issues. We came here as soon as we could to let you know in case you could stop them before they let it spread."

I put a hand to my collar and winced. The only thing I knew about The Fade had come from old fables my godmother mentioned long ago. The disease crept into one's brain and devoured them from the inside out.

"You! You're both the curse and the cure." Finn slowly backed away from me.

I extended my hands out in front of me, examining them for any signs of disease, but I'd vanished and returned back to Morningwood, and other than lingering grief, I felt fine. Granted, I was always a little bit of a mess in my head, but I didn't think I'd lost my mind. Not yet anyway.

"No, she's not a curse. She's a fucking dynamic force! According to Loure, he altered those sunflower seeds with a bit of everything. Penelope, you're unstoppable and probably even more so now that you're a vampire!" Fritzi said, reaching for my hand and squeezing it.

Her warm touch comforted me in the same way my godmother's had when I bruised a knee, my heart, or my ego.

"Time to shine, Princess. Isn't that right, Vail? This is going to make a great story once you capture that sample and destroy it. You're going to save the world. I just know it!" Henry clapped me on my back and tried to lighten the mood.

"That's not Vail. That's Finn." I swallowed the hard lump forming in my throat.

Mirror Mirror flashed my reflection back at me. It was the same one he'd shown me not long ago—the future me clad in black and wearing the blood of my enemies. I straightened my spine and gave him a curt nod.

Fritzi rose on her toes, scanning the hall behind us.

"Where's Vail?" she asked.

"He's gone. He and his brothers are meeting with The Council," I whispered before pushing past them and through the doorway.

Finn followed on my heels without a word.

"Wait! Where are you going?" Fritzi ran after us.

Trevor, Otto, and Grump scattered.

"To save my man, my brothers ... the world!" I called over my shoulder.

"Let me at least drive you!" She ran in front of me, opening the driver's door.

I nodded and slid into the passenger seat.

Finn barked orders at Grump and company to sound the

alarm and bring every loyal creature to The Cave or else The Crux would return to Morningwood. The group of misfits took off in the direction of the forest, howling, barking, and making a weird burping noise. I stuck my head out the window and burst out a quick song that assaulted my memory, echoing an ancient princess summons through the trees like a banshee calling my spirits home. The woods responded, shaking their leaves and returning my melody through a chorus of wolf howls, bear growls, owl hoots, and even a twinkling of fireflies rising from the treetops. Morningwood came alive.

"What the hell is all that racket?" Henry asked, jumping into the backseat with Finn.

"Just calling my family and friends for backup." I stretched the seat belt across my chest and buckled. "Now, drive."

Fritzi didn't hesitate despite the growing number of creatures emerging on the road ahead of us. She pushed her foot hard onto the pedal and burned a skid mark across the driveway before leaving Bostwick in our dust.

"I think you got your princessy qualities back," she said, hugging the curves in the road while dodging the stampeding animals near us.

"I think she's got more than that," Finn said from the backseat.

I clenched my jaw and fought off the thrill of bloodlust edging my heartless soul.

CHAPTER SIX

VAIL

WE PULLED INTO THE FIELD THAT LED TO THE CAVE'S entrance and parked underneath an ancient oak tree. Its gnarled, barren branches loomed overhead, nearly splitting in the gusty wind. A crack of thunder sliced through the quiet night. In the distance, the low rumble of music beckoned us to come and play.

"Here. Take two of these. You just pop them on your tongue and dissolve it with a bit of blood." Drake passed me a small jeweled case, decorated in amethysts and rubies.

I clicked open the top and shook out a handful of silver pills in my palm. They shimmered like diamonds, reflecting the flashes of lightning pouring through the windshield.

"Is this the pixie dust you spoke about?" I asked, separating two pills from the rest.

"It is. These are from volcanic pixies deep inside the earth. That's why they look like diamonds. It's the rarest form of dust on this side of the world," Drake said.

I handed Ian two and shoveled the rest back into the

container, minus the ones I put on the tip of my tongue. I reached for the bottle of demon's blood we'd passed around on the way over. I took a swig and swallowed the jewels, wiping the back of my hand across my mouth, leaving a rust-colored streak on my knuckles.

"Where did you find them?" I asked, giving the case back to Drake.

He took two pills, swallowing them dry before answering, "Best not to ask that."

I nodded, looking away. Garona stirred in the backseat between sips of Black Label. I'd given her the bottle before we left in hopes of distracting her from the tension in the air. But Penelope's clone was more intelligent than Finn had given her credit for—and even more so, she was stubborn. She twisted her mouth with the same far-off expression Penelope had when she became lost in her thoughts.

"No matter. Now's not the time to live like Bostwick brothers. We aren't here to cure vampirism and return to a more moral way of life. We're here to destroy, to kill, to finish. Tomorrow, we can rise again and continue our work for the cause. But tonight, we're vampires." I opened another bottle of blood and gulped half of it down before passing it to Ian. The warm liquid pooled in my belly, invigorating my energy to a level I hadn't felt in over a decade.

"I can't wait to finish these fuckers off. It'll be a new world, working without them breathing down our backs." Ian's pupils dilated. He chugged the remaining blood and threw the bottle on the floorboard with a growl.

Garona flinched and began to fidget with the laces on her dress. She hadn't mumbled a word since we'd left.

"No matter what happens tonight, remember, we've already won. We have the cure. It's safe at home. Let's keep it that way. Because tomorrow, we have the opportunity to walk in the sun and bring life back to our crypt."

The pixie dust sparked in my veins, bringing my senses cresting to a peak level I'd never experienced. Mayhem and bloodlust overtook my integrity, and for the first time in a long time, I let it. "This is it, boys—and girl. Let's give these vampires their hearts back and then rip them right out."

Garona punched the air with her fist before beating it against her chest with a growl.

"Ten! Ten!" she roared.

"Ten! Ten!" my brothers repeated, saluting each other.

"For Leo!" I saluted them back. "And for the cause!"

I exited the car and opened the back door, extending my hand for Garona. She clasped her manicured nails over my palm and smiled—the exact replica of my vampire princess back home.

"For Mowma." She pointed to the sky and shielded her eyes from the heavy raindrops pelting along her brow.

I opened my mouth to speak, but a chorus of howls from behind us interrupted, causing whatever thought I'd had to flee my mind.

"It's Antonio," Ian said, grabbing a case of Moondust from the trunk.

A pack of werewolves ran toward us, skidding to a halt at our feet and transforming into their human form.

"Vail. Ian. Drake. Penelope." Antonio nodded at each of us in greeting.

"Evenin'. You here to join our dinner meeting or what?" I moved closer to the tree trunk, ducking from the steadying drizzle of rain.

Antonio shook himself like a dog, sending water droplets flying in all directions. Ian threw his forearm in the air, blocking the spray of water.

"We're supposed to escort you to the door. But I have to warn you. The Council brought a guest." The wolf glanced toward Garona and back at me before stepping closer and whispering, "It's a princess."

"What?" I asked, unsure if I'd heard him correctly or if the pixie dust was beginning to play tricks on my ears.

"Yep. You heard me all right. She's of the sunflower variety too. I'm really sorry. I know you planned on using some decoy. I'm assuming that's her with you and not the real Penelope. Didn't tell my boys that." He glanced over his shoulder. "They're stressed enough as it is. We've been ordered to stand down unless provoked or given orders. We can't go inside with you. We have to patrol out here. But Bruno's guards are in there and waiting."

"So, those bastards are already here?" My fangs dripped with toxin.

"Yes. We had to escort them too. I don't want another repeat of the Bostwick Massacre. I hope you have a well-thought-out plan." He averted his eyes as Ian and Drake stuffed weapons in their waist and ankle holsters before covering them with their clothes.

"The plan's to kill them. Simple as that," I said, catching a knife Ian had tossed my way. I stuffed it in the back of my waistband and tightened my belt.

The wolves stirred behind us, casting a look of disapproval when they thought we weren't looking.

Antonio jerked his head toward The Cave, motioning for us to head that way. "Come on. Let's get this over with."

I took Garona by the elbow and ushered her to follow. She winced at my fingertips digging into her soft flesh.

"Sorry. It's the blood and dust. I didn't realize my own strength," I apologized and loosened my grip.

The rain slowed to a misty haze as we neared The Cave.

Ian and Drake trailed behind, carrying two cases of wine, one wrapped neatly with a bow.

Antonio stopped at a side door adjacent to The Cave's

entrance. It was nearly hidden, nestled into a giant boulder covered in a thin layer of moss. I'd been to The Cave plenty of times, but I didn't recognize this entry. I tuned my senses to the other side of the door but could hear nothing through the thick walls.

"We have to leave you here. This hall leads directly to the meeting area. Guards will be at the entry doors, so don't rush in there like madmen. Whatever your plan, it needs to be quick and stealthy. Bruno doesn't want to cause a scene. That's bad publicity," he said with a critical tone in his husky voice.

"Quick and stealthy," I repeated. "Good thing I'm all vampire."

Antonio shook his head and walked away. His pack quickly followed on his heels. The hair on the back of my neck stood on end as I picked up on the wolves' sense of dread.

"Listen up. They have a sunflower princess in custody. This doesn't change a thing. It's just a heads-up. Say no more, as I'm sure we're being watched. Let's go," I muttered under my breath, opening the door and directing them inside.

Ian and Drake shared a look of confusion before quickly composing themselves at the sound of a throat clearing.

"Good evening, gentlemen and Your Highness." Bruno stood a few paces down at a nearby door, guarded by two massive werewolves in their wolfish form. He rubbed his gold chain necklace between his thumb and index finger, stepping out from between the beasts. "I hope that's the wine I've heard about," he shouted. "The aliens won't shut up about it!"

I stopped in front of him and shook his hand. "Aye, it is. These are the last two cases. We won't have any more ready until next year." My voice echoed down the hall. The music from the dance club was barely audible through the thick cavern walls.

Bruno glanced behind him and snapped his fingers. "Fenric! Gus! Please come take these cases off our guests' hands."

A team of wolves emerged from the doorway and walked toward us, fetching the wine.

I lowered my voice, slipping a whisper out from between motionless lips. "Don't drink the wrapped one."

Bruno's draconian, slit eyes flashed for an instant before returning to normal. He spun on his heels and marched inside. "This way, please."

The crowded entrance opened into a meeting space much like the one we'd visited here previously. Silken tapestries hung from jagged rock walls, a different crest stitched across each one. I knew from the rumors I'd heard when I moved to Morningwood that they were collectibles from the kingdoms Bruno had destroyed centuries ago. Now, he preferred to lay low in the quiet company of his treasures, buried deep within the cavern.

My eyes quickly adjusted to the dim lighting, and I noticed the small group of vampires studying us. The Council had already been seated. Their pale skin glowed in the flickering candle flames spread across the narrow table. Charles, the head vampire, smirked, baring a chipped yellow fang. I strained against the rush of anger thundering through me and dipped my head in greeting.

Bruno walked toward the end of the table and directed us to sit. I put my hand on the small of Garona's back and led her to two empty chairs across from Charles. She buckled beside the table. On Charles's right sat a woman with the same honey-gold hair flowing down her back as Garona's. She stared down at her empty plate with the slightest tremble in her rosebud lips. A bead of sweat gathered across her brow. She looked like a slightly younger and more exotic Penelope.

"You all know each other, so I won't waste my time on introductions. But we do have a guest you might be familiar with, Penelope. This is Sabrina. She's from Romania, and according to The Council, she was also born from a sunflower." Bruno dropped down into his seat and sighed.

The Council observed Garona's reaction to Sabrina, but she only lifted her chin and gave a curt nod, barely acknowledging the woman across from her.

"And why bring her here? Is this another game of yours?" I asked, pulling Garona's chair out for her.

She gathered her dress in her hands and sat, smoothing the wrinkles out from under her. My brothers and I sat in the open spaces beside her. The pixie dust sparked in my veins, igniting a raw, defensive energy inside of me.

"We thought it'd be best these two meet before ... well, I hate to be so bold, but before we execute them entirely, burn their bodies, and make sure this golden bloodline never sees the light of day again. Get it?" A grin spread across Charles's jowls as he looked to his friends for approval.

The Council members' laughter coiled in my stomach.

"We're here to do our duty. Not play. Isn't it enough that you completely destroyed our business and killed our brother?" Drake stood, pressing his palms to the tablecloth and leaning across the candle centerpiece. His fangs hung low in his mouth, nearly piercing his bottom lip.

"Listen up," Bruno roared. "I agreed for this meeting here, so you both would be on neutral ground. The only reason I'm hosting is because my business is also suffering the fallout of your feud. No one wants to come to Morningwood anymore when they think they'll be caught in the middle of a vampire war. Our attendance in The Cave is down nearly half since the massacre. We're here tonight to finish it without trouble. My guards and I will make sure of it." A tendril of smoke escaped from between his lips.

"Understood. We won't be long. We're only here to bring her to you. But we're asking that you keep her in captivity and study her—not slaughter her or Sabrina. We want to hand her over, so you know we're done chasing this idea of curing vampirism. She was the cure. She's yours now. Just please don't hurt her. She's—"

Charles swiftly rose from his chair, knocking it behind him. He reached around his back and grabbed a blade before drawing it across Sabrina's neck. Her blood spilled down his knuckles, glowing from the candlelight in a shimmering waterfall of gold and garnet. She opened her mouth to speak but choked, dribbling a gurgle of blood from the corners of her lips. Two wolves rushed to restrain him, but the life had already left her eyes.

Beside me, Garona screamed.

"Damn it! I said, no drama!" Bruno roared a steady flame from his throat, scorching the planked table ashen black.

Everyone, except Garona, scooted back, nearly falling over in their chairs. She hung her head and reached out her hand, fumbling for my reassurance. I grabbed it and gave it the most comforting squeeze I could, but the lifeless squeeze she gave back told me she understood the level of danger we dined with.

"I'm sorry!" Charles put his hands in the air and struggled against the wolves' grips. "Look … we knew it was going to happen sooner or later. One down, one to go. I promise it won't be so sudden next time. I just need everyone to know I mean business. You don't want me to hurt her, yet you used her as a lab rat! Pfft. The Council has survived in Morningwood for three centuries. I won't let a little *princess* bring down what we've worked hard to build," he spat the words out with a sneer.

"And what's that? You do nothing. All you do is swing your little dicks around, scaring everyone like you're the kings of Morningwood. You don't contribute shit to anything. All you do is take, take, take." Ian leaned forward, clenching his jaw.

Charles let out a laugh and grabbed his crotch. "Little dick? That's hilarious. I'm a vampire. What do you expect from me? Goodwill and a motivational speech? Fuck no."

"Charles, no more of that shit, or I'll have you thrown out of here faster than you can take Penelope. Are we clear?" Bruno asked, drumming his fingers across the table.

Charles nodded, averting his eyes.

"Good. Let him sit," Bruno told the wolves.

Charles wiggled out of their grasp and sat back down, next to the dead princess.

"Gus, fill the glasses. We all need a drink. Open the Bostwick Moondust. What did you say it was made with, Ian? Fairy dust?" Bruno asked.

"Aye. From volcanic faeries. That's why it shines like diamonds." Ian's eyes flicked to Drake's before returning to Bruno.

"Actually, I'm not in the mood for wine. I brought a bottle of our own special drink. Daniel here's been making it for The League when they drop by to visit. You all remember The League, right?" Charles tilted his head at the bearded vampire on his left.

"What kind of drink?" I asked, licking my lips and refusing to betray my confidence.

Garona's knee shook underneath the table, knocking into mine.

"It's a craft cocktail. They're all the rage these days, don't you know? I'm sure Bruno has them in his bar." Charles looked at Bruno, but Bruno didn't respond. "Anywho, we call it Ambrosia. You know, like the nectar of the gods! We make it from night elf's blood, so you get that subtle earthy funk, like you would with red wine. But that's not what makes it special. It's special because it heightens your awareness to an entirely new level. One drink, and you can hear a twig snapping from the other side of the woods. I daresay we could all use that level of awareness tonight, hmm? You can trust me. This drink is my truce. Why else would I feed my enemies and strengthen their abilities?"

Drake side-eyed me and subtly shook his head.

"How thoughtful—and daring." Bruno breathed out a plume of smoke. "Let's have a taste."

Daniel rose from his seat and lumbered toward a bag on the floor beside the entry. He squatted down, rifling through it until he found a large glass bottle twice the size of one of our bottles of wine. The liquid inside glowed a desolate blue—the same color of night-elf skin. One of the guards grabbed the bottle from his hand and inspected it.

"It's night elf's blood. That's why it's glowing." Daniel yanked the bottle back from the werewolf's hands. "Do you think we'd be so dumb as to put poison in your drinks? That's a bit obvious, isn't it?"

"Bruno, can you call off your mutts? This paranoia is getting to be a bit ridiculous." Charles shifted in his seat and blew out a breath.

"They're my guards, and you'll respect them in my lair. We agreed that this is neutral ground. I'm not picking sides. But you're making it difficult. My guards are here to protect me—not you and not Bostwick. If they want to inspect your fucking alcohol, they're going to inspect your fucking alcohol." Bruno pushed himself up from the table and began to pace the room. His shoulders began to grow, bursting the seams of his dinner jacket.

The wolves circled the table.

"I invite you all into my home to clear the air, and this is how you repay me," Bruno hissed, flashing his forked tongue. "I've got a dead princess at my dinner table, soaking in a pool of her own damn blood; a questionable glowing blue liquid in the hands of dirty, lying vampires; and a group of brothers hiding who knows how many guns and knives underneath their suits."

Charles shot a glare in my direction. I met his gaze and smirked, peeling back the left side of my dinner jacket and revealing a pistol and two knives nestled inside a holster. He shrugged, looked down at his watch, and smiled. The crowd on the other side of the wall grew louder, drowning out the rapid heartbeats I'd heard pounding throughout the room. Even Bruno, one of the world's most ancient dragons, couldn't slow his thundering pulse. We hadn't even dined, and the tension in the air had already become unbearable.

"Dirty vampires, eh?" Charles's curt voice lashed out. "You let them in here with weapons but didn't trust us? We're The Council. We rule Morningwood, and you dare disrespect us like that, lizard boy? You don't know what you're saying. You see, I was going to try to do this the easy way. But it looks like you've left me no choice." He stuffed a hand inside his pants pocket.

Two wolves flew across the room, knocking Charles off of his feet. But the vampires next to him sprang into action, pulling syringes from inside their jackets and jabbing them into the wolves' thick coats. They let out a howl and reverted to human form, contorting their bodies into painful shapes.

"What the fuck was that?" Bruno roared. His eyes turned a sickly shade of reptilian yellow. Black scales crept up from his shirt collar, slowly spreading across his face. His nails curved outward into piercing talons.

I reached for my pistol.

"I was going to demonstrate on your princess and show

you all, but these bastards will have to do." Charles kicked one of the wolves in the side.

The wolf curled into a limp ball, unable to fight back. A vacant stare shadowed his eyes.

"It's The Fade. And at those high doses, I'm afraid they might have five minutes to live before they lose their minds and maul each other to death. Pity. Who's next?" Charles rubbed his palms together and showed his fangs.

The other Council members rose from their seats, ready to pounce.

"You." Ian pulled a pistol from his back and pulled the trigger, aiming for Charles's head.

But The Council leader bent his body backward, dodging it before I could blink.

"I told you that you should have drunk Ambrosia. I know you're regretting it now!" Charles threw his head back and laughed.

Drake brandished two weapons and pointed them at the vampires on either side of Charles.

"Get them!" Bruno commanded.

The wolves rushed by in a blur, tackling the vampires. Drake managed to land a bullet in one of the member's chests before the member fell to the ground under the beast. His body quickly withered away to a pile of hot ash.

"Wooden bullets," Drake said, shooting me a smile before barrel-rolling out of the way of another attacker. He swerved on his feet, leaped through the air, and avoided any altercation with a skill set I'd never seen him use.

I tore my gaze from my impressive brother and spoke quickly, "Hide underneath here. Stay put and don't move." I ducked, grabbing Garona, and shoved her under the table.

She rocked back and forth, clutching her knees to her chest and wailing. I cursed Finn for not testing her emotions before he coded her alive. With every advancement she'd made, a stab of guilt buried inside my chest. I wasn't supposed to struggle with these emotions, and neither was she. But Penelope's blood had brought a taste of life to us both.

"Come play, lizard boy! I've always wanted to see what The Fade can do to a dragon. I bet you aren't so powerful after all."

I popped my head back up to see Charles waving a syringe in the air, beckoning Bruno. The dragon took the bait, rising up into his final form and lashing his teeth at two vampires before swallowing them whole.

The sound of stampeding footsteps barreled down the hall as ten more Council members flew into the room, followed by a pack of barking wolves. I glanced in their direction and pulled the gun from my side, shooting two of the vampires and slowing their entrance. Across the room, Ian straddled Daniel, crunching his fist against his enemy's face until he left nothing of it, except a mess of blood and bone.

Garona let out a low, husky growl, pointing behind me, but her warning came too late. I took a series of massive blows to the back of my head and fell on my knees, dropping my weapon. My vision blurred as I rolled on my back, desperately trying to focus on where the hits were coming from. When my eyes finally adjusted to my surroundings, The Council member stood, looming over me with a syringe held tight in his grip.

"That's right. Wake up, asshole! I want you coherent when I stab this needle into your worthless soul. You didn't want to be a vampire anymore, so here's your chance. Now, you'll just be another tortured piece of shit until you die an agonizing death or disappear entirely. Poof. Gone. Ashes to ashes." He snorted, swinging his arm down to my chest.

"No!" Garona leaped from underneath the table and covered my body.

He sank the needle deep into her back, shattering through her rib cage.

"No! No! No! Fuck!" I pulled from my anxious strength and rolled her off of me and onto her back.

The light in her eyes dulled.

"I ten-ten," she croaked before vanishing completely.

"Huh. I guess that's what it does to a princess." The vampire scratched his head before Ian put a bullet through his skull, bursting it into shards raining down on me like shrapnel.

I brushed a splintered bit of brain from my cheek and growled.

"Come on," he yelled, running to help me up.

I scrambled to my feet and threw myself into the action, burying my fangs into a vampire's neck until I felt his spine snap. I drew the blade from my holster and gutted the next vampire who flew at me. The wolves grew ferocious, tearing limbs from The Council and clasping their jaws around the members' fragile skulls. Drake sprang backward, sending a round of shots through the air and narrowly missing a wolf. The wolf howled, reprimanding him, but our vampire senses had kicked in, and everything in our path became fair game.

The ground shook beneath me, drawing my attention to the dragon across the room. He stumbled on his talons, and a roaring stream of fire flowed from his mouth, heating the air to a sticky temperature. A group of vampires surrounded him, jabbing syringes through his thick scales until he collapsed with a loud thud. Our forces dwindled along with any hope I'd had left. The Council had overtaken the wolves, a dragon, and Bostwick. Our devious plans had burned up in a barrel of flames.

Charles's laughter became maniacal.

"Too easy! You're all making this too easy!" he yelled.

"Drake! Ian!" I screamed, calling my brothers to me for a final good-bye, but the needle that pierced through my chest silenced me from speaking further.

"I'm going to let you suffer." Charles sauntered toward me, smiling as my body began to convulse.

I tossed and turned across the stone floor, fighting the fuzzy zaps in my brain that flooded my thoughts with terrifying visions. Penelope's head rested on a spike atop Morningwood Manor. Gertie lay dead in Priscilla's cage. And my brothers' ashes scattered in the wind, blowing back to the winery, which was burning to ruins. I moaned, wrestling off the horrible thoughts assaulting my mind before my world turned black and empty.

CHAPTER SEVEN

PENELOPE

As Fritzi sped down the gravel roads, I grabbed the door handle and pushed myself deep into my seat. The Cave sat, tucked into an enchanted field out in the middle of nowhere, clouded by a heavy mist that never let up, shielding shenanigans from the naked human eye. The bustling night-club frequently hosted the South's most notorious para-normal events, drawing in supernatural from all over the world. Otherwise known to the locals as The Bogeyman, Bruno had cultivated a booming business and a massive cash flow by simply providing a place for weirdos to be weirdos. But to me, the club was just another spot for trouble.

"I need to know more about The Fade and what Loure said he altered Penelope with. Did he mention the extent of her power?" Finn leaned forward, sticking his head between Fritzi and me.

"He didn't say. Honestly, he didn't tell me much about The Fade, or The Crux, or whatever, except what it could do to humans and vampires. He talked about Priscilla mostly.

He did mention a vital part about the disease, which is the turning point. That's why it's called The Crux. I didn't quite understand it, but I guess it's something about …" Fritzi twisted her mouth upward.

"A vampire's choosing. When the body is in that pivotal moment of transformation, the brain and body each make a choice. It's when they disagree that The Crux happens." Finn sat back in his seat and rolled the window down, letting in a blast of night air and misting rain.

"Yes! That's it!" She pointed her finger in the air. "So, how is it contagious if you have a choice?"

"You don't. The Crux happens naturally—kind of like cancer in humans. But if you're injected or if the disease somehow gets into your blood system via a bite, wound, or whatever, then you become positively infected. Otherwise, it's the luck of the draw, and the unlucky ones contract it naturally," Finn said, rubbing his palms into his eye sockets. "I can't believe I never thought about this when you were fading, Penelope. I'm so damn sorry. I just thought it was some princess thing. I didn't know the damn plague had come back."

I stared ahead, not bothering to turn and face him. A group of deer leaped alongside our car, followed by a swooping flock of birds. I side-eyed Fritzi, who drove, clutching the steering wheel with both hands, focusing on staying directly inside the yellow street lines. If she veered an inch right or left, she'd barrel our vehicle into a pack of wild animals.

"What's done is done. Maybe this new information can help us, moving forward." I squeezed my eyes shut and shuddered. The blood in my veins slowly began to pulse.

"Well, if you're mixed with other powers, there truly is no stopping you. Your abilities keep mutating almost daily. I saw what you did with the bird. That means, you have white-witch capabilities. We've seen your dark magic and princess stuff. I know you can read and translate memories because of the moonshine-and-demon fiasco. I bet you could even stop time if you wanted—or at least slow it, like some demons do. Hell, The Fade is kind of similar to time travel. I've studied both." Finn droned on about the DNA sequencing of the disease.

Fritzi turned the corner to the field, jumping a curb and rolling through a tall thicket of thorns and vines. A dull heartbeat sprang inside my chest, startling my nerves. I rubbed my breastbone and gasped.

"Why's my heart beating, Finn? What ability is that from? Am I turning human? I have a pulse!" I opened my eyes and pressed my fingertips to my temples, warding off a sudden wave of nausea.

"What? Lean back!" Finn reached around the backseat and put his palm to my chest. He bolted upright, jerking his hand back. "I'm not sure how that's possible. You didn't drink anything, did you? Did you test that moonshine Ian had made? The one with your blood?"

"No! Why would I risk that?" A tingling sensation gathered in my toes and fingertips.

"What about any Project X or blood? Have you fed?" His voice rose to an almost-inaudible pitch.

"No! I drank … I drank from Vail. It was during a moment, and I bit him. That's all!" The sudden realization that my love bite might have been a bad idea caused my legs to tremble.

Fritzi skidded to a stop at the back of an overgrown and crowded parking lot. The forest creatures rushed ahead, stampeding into The Cave in angry swarms.

"That's not your heartbeat then. It's Vail's. He's turning." Finn scrambled out of the car and opened my door, urging me out.

But my body seized, unable to move.

"Bite me!" Fritzi shoved her wrist into my face.

My stomach seized with the ache of hunger. She smelled like sunshine, daisies, and warm milk.

"Do it now. You need the energy! It's just like taking a shot of whiskey. Bottoms up! I trust you to save us."

I trailed my eyes down her shoulder and fixated my gaze on her wrist. A tiny pulse fluttered underneath her pale skin, luring me into biting my friend.

"Wait!" Henry called from the backseat, jumping forward.

My chest began to wither into an erratic rhythm.

"Bite me! I've got genie blood! Or I used to!" He thrust his neck into my mouth. "Maybe it can—"

I sank my teeth deep into his neck before he could finish his thought, gulping down the hot liquid until it scorched my throat.

Fritzi drew in a sharp breath and reached for her husband. "Careful. Please don't hurt him."

I pulled back and swiped my thumb across my mouth, wiping away a dribble of blood. Her husband tasted like patchouli, but his blood worked like magic.

"Go to the winery and hide in the underground lab beneath Finn's desk. It's in the basement. The keypad is on the wall by the door. Finn, give her the code!" I commanded.

Finn wrung his hands and stalled, looking toward The Cave and back at me again.

"Finn!" I yelled, bursting the windows from the car.

Shards of glass flew at my face before slowing to a stop. I reached out and flicked a jagged piece from the air before it hit Fritzi's nose. The rest of the splinters turned to water droplets, falling to the ground as soon as time caught back up to whatever the fuck I'd done.

"I knew you could stop time." Finn fell to his knees and began to cough. Water beaded down his hairline, dripping into his thick brows. "It's nine, zero, one, five, seven, six." He heaved.

Henry rubbed the wound on his neck and jumped into the passenger seat as I toppled out, pulling Finn to his feet. Fritzi stared out of the windowless car and nodded, repeating the lab's code.

"Good luck, Princess. You're going to do just fine." Henry's voice wavered, hardly audible over the commotion ahead.

I clenched my jaw and gave them a curt nod before Finn and I ran off in the opposite direction. My stomach lurched over the sickening sounds escaping the caverns. Crowds trampled each other, falling into bloodied piles at the club's entry. Dead bodies were scattered outside, facedown in muddy puddles. A goat lay on his back with all four hooves in the air, already dead and bloated.

"Grump!" I screamed, rushing toward him.

"Princess! It's not me. It's not me!" Grump hiccuped from underneath a nearby truck beside me.

I stooped down to see my family shivering together in a huddle. Otto held his broken wing.

"You all need to get back home! It's too dangerous here."

"We tried to fight. We really did! But a dirty, drunken troll stumbled and grabbed Otto's wing to try to steady himself. The dumb bastard just fell over, taking Otto and his wing with it. We can't leave him behind." Grump sobbed. Mud and wine were caked throughout his billy-goat scruff.

Trevor moved in front of Otto, shielding him with his tail.

"No, of course not. No one gets left behind. Stay here, and I'll get you when it's safe. I have to find Vail." I whispered the first incantation to pop into my head and disguised the truck as the giant pink taco truck I'd seen Henry frequent.

"How's this help?" Grump asked.

"It's going to be too late if we don't go now!" Finn shot me a thunderous expression.

"I don't know, but something just told me it would!" I hurried to my feet and took off into The Cave, pulling Finn along behind me.

"The fuck!" came a loud voice from inside the truck. A tattooed woman peeked out of the side window before quickly disappearing back inside. "Ah, hell no! Nikki, you picked up the wrong juju crystal!"

"I can feel his heartbeat. It's stronger here!" I swerved through the crowds until we reached a carelessly abandoned doorway on the side of the cavern. Its door hung from a broken hinge.

"Then, he's inside. You're connected with him, like he was when he fed on you. Fuck! I hope Ian and Drake haven't turned." His words came out in a rush, barely decipherable.

I wasn't sure if Finn had ever had to fight. His skills excelled in a lab, not on the battlefield.

We flew down a rocky path toward the end of the hall, hurdling over a slain Council member. The emblem stitched across his chest charred at the edges as he slowly disintegrated into a pile of ash. Up ahead, two mangled wolf corpses blocked a doorway.

"He's in there." I paused, peering into a chaotic scene, similar to what I'd witnessed during the Bostwick Massacre. The haunting memory of that night overtook me, washing over me with sudden, vengeful wrath.

I gathered my dress in my hands and stepped over the wolves and into my worst nightmare.

"Enough!" I screamed, rolling my voice through the air like a clap of thunder. It hit the back of the cavern, echoing back into a deafening shrill.

The vampires and wolves stopped mid-fight, pressed their palms to their ears, and collapsed to the floor.

"I said, enough!" I repeated. The force of my voice shook the cave, sending bits of rock and dust crumbling from the ceiling.

The vampires moaned, crawling along the floor toward the exit. The two wolves left alive whimpered, clambering to get to each other.

I strolled deeper inside, scanning the room for Vail and his brothers, but stopped in my tracks at the sight of a sister princess lying, slumped over in a chair. The gaping wound in her neck glistened with the honey-hued blood drying on her laced collar. Flecks of gold still oozed from her slit throat, but her eyes were long since dead.

"Who did this?"

The ground beneath me shook. Finn flew off to my right, stooping to help his brothers. My heart thumped with a rough rhythm beneath my rib cage, sending a shot of adrenaline through my gut. In the corner, an old, portly vampire crouched next to Bruno. The dragon lay, splayed on his belly, with his forked tongue rolled to the side. An empty void, much like the princess's, reflected from his eyes.

"I knew those Bostwick assholes had something up their sleeves. So, the real you didn't vanish, eh? Or did you just come back?" The Council man stood, scratching his head. He centered his focus on a nearby vampire lying beside the dinner table. "What did you do?" His nostrils flared.

"Vail!" I tore my gaze from the mouthy Council member and rushed to Vail's side, kneeling before him.

Streaks of blood and ash were smeared across his face like war paint. I gritted my teeth and fought back the urge to be sick. Ian, Drake, and Finn crashed down next to us.

"Did they inject you?" I asked, sweeping my hands over his body in search of evidence that he'd been jabbed.

He gave a ragged breath and heaved as his life quickly slipped through my fingers.

"Bite him," Finn urged. "Now!"

I glanced around the room, assessing my situation in a panic. The remaining vampires had pinned themselves against the wall. At the entry, a group of beastly forest creatures blocked their paths. There wasn't an escape. We'd all die here.

I stared at the last Council member making his way toward us in a huff of anger and sank my teeth into Vail's collar, releasing my bitter toxin into his bloodstream. I trusted Finn knew enough about my DNA and what it might do to Vail if I bit him.

"Fucking bitch! You bit him! Now, what do you think it will do to you?" The Council member bellowed, stomping toward me. "You're going to disappear from our world! Imbecile. Don't you know The Council could do great things with your blood?"

I groaned, pushing my grief for Garona out of my thoughts and exchanging it for the raw bloodlust I'd refused to give in to once I became a vampire. Whatever innocent, princessy qualities still lurking inside my dead body were squashed by a vicious need to kill. The heartbeat inside of me hitched, skipping in a familiar rhythm—*one, two, three. One, two, three, three.*

I jerked my head upright and stuck my palm out, sending a quick burst of wind toward the asshole vampire, sending him flying backward through the air. His skull hit the ground with a thud. I rushed to my feet and ran toward him, repeatedly kicking my leather boot into his ribs until I heard a crack. It only took three kicks before I rendered him immobile.

He gasped, a dark liquid bubbling from his mouth. The animals at the entry stirred, but the rest of the room fell silent. Finn and his brothers dragged Vail off to the side.

"You think you can get rid of us this easily?" The vampire

rolled to his hands and knees, coughing splattered drops of blood across the stone floor.

I put my boot to the back of his head and smashed his face into the rock, grinding his skull into the cavern floor. He began to let out a muffled scream, calling for the other members to help. But one glance over my shoulder, and they remained in place.

"Maul them," I whispered, commanding the hungry beasts in the hall and permitting them entrance.

Three bears lazily lumbered inside, making their way toward the leftover Council members. A group of snakes slithered across the floor toward the vampires' feet. Wildcats slunk from the back, readying themselves to pounce. A swarm of bees circled the vampires before the revolting screams started. The forest creatures began to tear my enemies to shreds, slowly savoring the satisfaction of ending their reign in Morningwood—their woods, our home. The vampires fought back, but they were severely outnumbered. It was no use.

I returned my gaze to the vampire on the floor and rolled him over with my foot so that he could see my smile.

"What are you?" he sputtered out between slivers of teeth and fangs piercing through his bottom lip.

A look of unrelenting malice reflected from his eyes before I realized that reflection was me.

"I'm your new queen," I answered with a curtsy, sending a flock of doves out from beneath my dress.

They swooped down, pecking his eyes from their sockets and drowning his screams with each rapid beat of their wings.

One, two, three. One, two, three, three.

His body combusted into a ball of flames, rising in a narrow tendril of black smoke. I flicked my wrist and cleared the air. Behind me, the wild animals still fed upon my victims.

"Let's go home," a familiar voice said, placing his hand along my shoulder.

His comforting touch shocked me back to reality. I turned around and fell into Vail's nook, silently crumbling inside. He pressed his vacant chest to mine and held me tight as I choked back racking sobs. Whatever heartbeat he'd gained from The Crux had vanished.

"Garona?" I asked, pulling back and inspecting him at arm's length.

His skin was the same pale shade I'd always known, and his eyes weren't darkened any more than usual. He was every bit of the man I'd met back in the forest, without any sign of humanity or deadly vampire. He was just Vail, a mysterious species all his own.

"I'm so sorry." He shook his head.

I nodded, swallowing a lump in my throat.

"There's nothing left for us here then." I swiped a hand across the air and dismissed my forest friends.

The ragged beasts filtered outside, leaving The Cave in dead silence. Ian and Finn shuffled toward us. Drake limped along behind them.

"We have to get back to Fritzi and Henry," Finn said.

"Fritzi and Henry?" Vail asked.

"They're staying at the winery. They drove us." I kneaded the back of my shoulder.

"What about Bruno and the other bodies? We can't just leave them here," Drake said, sweeping his palms out toward the mess of corpses littering the floor.

"I'm not dead, assholes." Bruno's voice grew gruff as he rose to his claws. "It's a trick I picked up from my guards—play dead. Besides, I want that bastard, Captain Tuttle's, treasures too much to leave this world without them."

I ran toward the dragon and tried to stop him from overexerting himself, but he only laughed, blowing out a wispy flame.

"Their needles didn't even prick through one scale. I'm fine. But my wolves … not so much."

He scanned the room. A few wolves whimpered, pawing themselves up on their hind legs and reverting to humans.

"If there are any members of that damn cult left, you make sure to bring them to me."

"I think we got them all." Ian brushed his hands together.

"Maybe, maybe not. We had someone stalking the winery. That's why we need to get back now," Finn reminded me.

"Shit. Fritzi!" I said, gripping my waist at the pang of terror punching my gut.

"Let's go." Vail took my hand, pulling me along behind him.

I never looked back.

We emerged from the pits of hell to a desolate field. The clouds had parted, revealing a half-moon hanging low in the distance. Dozens of empty bottles and cups lay, scattered across the muddy grass, in between more bodies than I could count. My fox, gargoyle, and goat friends were still huddled underneath a broken spell. The pink taco truck had disappeared, leaving my friends exposed to whatever evil lurked in the shadows.

"Otto!" I rushed toward my pet gargoyle and gently scooped him into my arms, taking care not to touch his injured wing.

He curled his spine, burying his fat head into my chest, and whimpered. His skin felt like worn leather.

"It's going to be all right," I assured him.

His body grew limp in my hands. Beside me, Vail hoisted Grump over his shoulder like a sack of laundry.

"Hey! I'm not a big chunk of ham you can sling around. You ain't taking me to the slaughterhouse, are you?" Grump asked. "Because I hind-kicked one of those vampires clear across this field. I really did. Tell him, Trevor."

The fox twitched his whiskers and looked away. A deep gash had been cut above his furry brow.

"I believe you. We aren't taking you to slaughter. But we have to get back to the winery now. Fritzi's in danger," I said, following behind Ian.

"Who?" Grump asked from behind Vail's shoulder as he bobbed along with us.

"Fritzi, my friend. Don't you remember her, or did you get blackout drunk when we had that convo?"

"Eh … maybe."

Ian stopped in front of the car and opened the back door, ushering us inside. We stuffed ourselves in the back while Drake eased himself into the front passenger seat, swinging his right leg into the car with his hands.

"It's broke, but I can set it," Finn said.

Drake only nodded in response.

Ian started the engine and pressed the gas pedal to the floor, speeding off in the direction of the winery before we got settled. "How did you know they had The Crux?" he asked.

"Long story short, we received an upright Tower tarot card in the mail slot shortly after Penelope brought a bird back to life. Then, Fritzi and her husband, Henry, showed up at our doorstep. They'd met with Priscilla's ex-husband, Loure. He's in the human world. He spilled the beans about everything and told Fritzi that Priscilla had the last sample of the disease left. Fritzi put two and two together and came to warn us," Finn said while inspecting Otto's wing.

The gargoyle burst into tears.

"I'll fix yours too; don't worry." Finn patted Otto on the head.

"Wait. Back up. Did you say Penelope brought back a bird?" Vail asked, tugging his earlobe.

"Yep. She can explain more later ... after my story. I have some explaining to do too." He let out a long-drawn-out sigh.

"What did you do?" Drake turned in his seat, baring his fangs and wincing.

"Nothing! Damn!" Finn threw his hands in the air and pushed himself further into the backseat.

"We can speak about whatever later. Right now, the most important thing is to make sure Fritzi and Henry are okay and then make sure there aren't any Council members left. How many do you think were at the winery?" Vail asked.

"I sensed two. Maybe three." I shifted my feet, unable to find any level of comfort, squashed between my hulking vampire boyfriend and the car door.

"So, they wanted to send a message first. How nice." An edge of bitterness cut into Vail's words.

"Do you think Fritzi and Henry could handle them? I told them to hide in the secret-secret lab. You know, the one under Finn's desk? He gave them the code," I asked.

Finn cleared his throat and cracked a window, letting in the frigid night air. His frown drooped lower, loosening his jaw.

"If they're in my lab, they'll be fine. Nothing in there will harm them, and it's completely locked down. It's the safest space in Morningwood. I made damn sure of that," Finn said, snapping his eyes to mine.

I rested my head against the window and closed my eyes, imagining Fritzi and Henry climbing down to safety inside Finn's lab, only to find his corpse bride awaiting them. I didn't have the energy to reveal Finn's secret to the brothers just yet. They'd find out soon enough.

"I hope so. They have a baby to get home to." I fluttered open my eyes and caught Vail watching me.

His brows pulled together before he brushed a spider from my shoulder. It fell to my lap and scurried to the floor, leaving a bright silver webbed trail behind. It was the same enchanted webbing that had hung in the corners and crevices of Morningwood Manor.

CHAPTER EIGHT

VAIL

I LEFT THE ANIMALS IN THE CAR UNDER DRAKE'S CARE AND burst through the winery's door, closest to the laboratory. Finn, Ian, and Penelope followed on my heels. The doors were locked, and the grounds were empty of any frightening clues. But a hint of danger lingered in the air, tingling against my senses, still switched on high alert from the dust.

We flew downstairs toward the cellar, knocking over anything in our wake until the sharp and dizzying scent of gasoline whirled through the stairwell, slowing my steps.

"No." Finn shook his head, pushing me into the wall and barreling past.

Ian and I exchanged glances before running after him.

"Fritzi!" Penelope called. "Fritzi! Henry!"

She reached the bottom of the stairs and paused, but only a deafening silence met her pleas.

"Guys?" Finn rushed down the hall and pushed open the laboratory door, stepping inside.

The lab looked the same as it had the night of the massacre, except the intruders had left nothing untouched this time. The broken cold case used to store our samples was shattered across the gasoline-covered floor. Someone had smashed Finn's computers, files, and machines into a mangled mess. The cot in the corner lay, overturned, its metal legs bent, as if someone had repeatedly slammed it against the wall.

Finn fell on his knees with a gut-wrenching scream.

"Look!" Penelope stumbled into the room and pointed at a trail of blood leading around the corner and into the office.

"Stay back." Ian motioned, drawing his weapon and pinning himself against the wall.

Penelope and I kept silent, but the princess's fingertips crackled and glowed with electric energy. Finn still sat, collapsed on the tiles, as if he'd already given up hope for whatever the fuck he had hidden beneath the floor. I reached for a broken bottle beside me and clutched its neck in my palm. A shock of adrenaline burst inside my chest, revitalizing the bloodlust that had faded on the drive back home.

Ian slid his body sideways one step at a time before peeking into the office.

"Clear," he said, lowering his weapon and beckoning us to him.

Inside the room, a few random tarot cards lay beside two piles of ash, smoldering atop a puddle of oozing blood. Ian and I quickly ran over and stomped them out, splashing ash, gasoline, and blood all over ourselves. Finn shuffled to his feet and stood frozen in the doorway.

"Open your lab," I commanded, pointing my finger at him with a fury I'd reserved for too many years.

He'd kept his secrets long enough, and this time, whatever the fuck he'd created down there could have killed Penelope's friends. I refused to have any hint of danger lurking around Bostwick anymore.

Finn nodded, dragging his feet to the keypad on the wall. His fingers flew across the keys, typing in his secret code— the same one he'd refused to give to anyone else. Once I'd discovered Garona, I'd thought that he didn't have any secrets left to hide.

But from what little information Leo had told me long ago, I knew Finn was a mad scientist at heart, and his excited ideas harbored no limits. His curious nature led him to more secrets and more trouble than he could handle. But Leo had seen something more in Finn and saved him from whatever hell Finn had gotten himself mixed up in. Once Leo had convinced Finn to help us cure vampirism, he'd ordered everyone to give up their suspicions and quit questioning Finn's theories and experiments. We all had jobs at Bostwick. Finn's had always been the most important. We were to protect him—and his work—with our vampire lives.

Penelope twisted her hands, backing away from the trap-door underneath his desk. The muscle in her jaw flinched with each moment that passed while she waited for her friends' fate. I took two strides and stood next to her, placing my palm on her back. The air around her crackled, causing my hair to stand on end. I buzzed with her contagious energy as the door slid open, hissing through its vacuum seal.

"It's about damn time!" Fritzi popped her head from the hole in the ground and climbed out. "We've been hiding in here ever since Henry managed to stab a broken broomstick through those two vampires! He got lucky—that's for damn sure—because those beasts were ferocious!"

Henry groaned behind her. "Just because I'm no longer a genie doesn't mean I can't handle my own!"

"Fritzi!" Penelope rushed to her side and threw her arms around her. "You're okay?"

Henry brushed his hands down his pant legs and stretched. "Aye, we're okay. I'm afraid your lab isn't."

"Downstairs?" Finn clutched his chest and hurried toward the ladder.

I climbed down after him.

"What is it that's so important down here? I don't get it. Do you have some secret superpower ability you're working on? Creating some type of superhero? What are you hid—" My voice caught in my throat as I jumped off the ladder and landed, facing a half-naked corpse strapped to a table and standing upright.

Finn stood beside her, holding her limp arm in his hand, examining her from head to decrepit toe.

"I'll show you," Finn said, calling me over. His eyes sparked alive.

I made my way to his side on cautious feet, taking in my surroundings and preparing for a sinister surprise. But nothing other than the dead body lying in front of me seemed out of the ordinary for a laboratory. Beakers of frothy liquid decorated the countertops, and more computers and machines blinked from a corner table. I shivered, shaking off a sickening feeling as I neared the dead woman. Her long red hair flowed neatly down her shoulders, as if someone had carefully brushed it into place.

The conversation upstairs grew animated and nearly hysterical. But I couldn't make out any words. My thoughts were elsewhere as I mentally struggled to come to terms with a brother who had lost his mind.

"Vail, this is my fiancée. She's been dead for decades. She died right before Leo found me. He knew about her and promised I could ... work on her here while I also worked on the cure. I want to bring her to life." Finn dropped his gaze and gently trailed his fingertips over her knuckles before squeezing her hand.

"Like Frankenstein? You're trying to make a monster?" I stepped back.

"No! She's not a monster. She was human. I'm trying to turn her into a vampire, so we can be together forever. I never really wanted to cure vampirism for myself. I wanted to do it for the cause, so I could also utilize DNA and whatever else I could to fix this—fix her," he said, wrinkling his brow.

"Who did this to her?" I tilted my chin at the long scar that stretched from her collar down to her breastbone, disappearing underneath her bra.

Her ghastly, pale skin glistened with some type of oily barrier.

"I did."

I sucked in a breath through my fangs and prickled at his guilty admission.

"But not like that. I tried to … well, my fiancée and I had a *theory*. We called it the Heartless Theory. We believed the heart is much more than an organ. It can still live inside of us, like a spirit … or the soul. Maybe it is the soul. They are one and the same. It's hard to explain." He scratched his head, rolling his eyes to the ceiling.

"I've had that thought too. Go on." I nodded.

"Anyway, she worked with me at the lab. We wanted to test the theory, and our experiment went wrong. The Council … they fucked it all up. They tricked me. One of them anyway. I had done some work with him, and it's a long story. He's dead now. But so is she." He returned his gaze to mine.

"And you think you can really bring her back?" I rubbed the back of my neck and swallowed, unable to tear my attention from the stricken look etched in his fiancée's face.

"You know how I've been testing all those hearts in jars? I've been trying to make them beat for her and us. I've not had any luck. The closest I've come was writing a program like I did for Garona."

A heavy silence fell between us. It was too early for me to acknowledge the clone's passing.

"So, you've been hiding your dead fiancée inside here this whole time? Why didn't you tell me?" I quickly changed the topic.

"Because you'd have thought I'd lost my mind! Do you have any idea the amount of work required to keep her body from decomposing? It's under a mixture of so many balms, spells, and charms that if she wakes up, she might already be halfway to becoming a witch." He threw his hands in the air and walked off toward a shelf, plucking a jarred heart from the top.

"You're right about that. I would have thought you'd lost your mind if I hadn't met Penelope. But I understand love now. I would have done it too. I think." I chewed my bottom lip and contemplated the lengths I would go to for my lover.

He brought the jar to me and placed it in my hands. "It's hers. I've kept it all these years. I can't get it to beat again, but oddly enough, I'm still connected to her. I know that doesn't make sense. But I fed off of her, and though she never turned me human, as Penelope did with you, I still felt her presence when she was nearby, even after her death. Sometimes, when I'm in a deep, peaceful state, like asleep, I can feel her. For a long time, she communicated with me in different ways but mostly in dreams. I slept most of my time away before I began experimenting again, just so I could see her face. I still do."

"Does she continue to communicate then?" I handed the jar back to him.

"It's slowed … a lot. But I think if Penelope could bring that little bird back, maybe she can bring her back too." His voice trailed off into a hopeful whisper.

"A bird is a lot different than an entire human. We don't even know what Penelope's capable of. She could lose or gain more powers by the minute. We'll have to test her pre-vampire blood and maybe duplicate it, so we have enough to figure out your zombie-bride situation too. Is that possible? To duplicate it?" I shifted my weight on my feet.

The conversation above us echoed lively energy down the hole.

Finn rubbed his palms against his eye sockets and blew out a long breath.

"Her blood was up there." He turned his face up and pinched the bridge of his nose. "The last of it was destroyed. I planned on bringing it down here tonight, but Fritzi and Henry got here before I could return to my lab, and then the next thing I knew, I was in the car with Penelope. Fuck. I'm sorry. I can try and work with what we have now—her vampire blood. But it's an entirely different beast and could take ages to manually re-sequence, if that's even possible."

"Are you saying, we have no cure?" I put my hand out on a table behind me, steadying myself. The rush of panic that hit me was worse than the night's trauma in The Cave.

"I'm saying, we have to work with what we've got. Whatever Penelope is now, not what she was. It's not a cure, but she obviously fixed you with her toxin." Finn tried—and failed—to lift my spirits.

"But I'm dead. I'm still not human."

"Exactly. It's not a cure."

"I don't know what to say," I said, crumbling at the thought of telling Penelope our hopes and dreams had vanished and burned—the common fate of vampires everywhere.

"Neither do I." He reached for his fiancée's head and smoothed her hair back.

I turned to leave him alone with his project and relay the

bitter news to the one person in Morningwood who didn't deserve to hear it. She'd spent so much of her time and energy helping our cause, only for us to fail it and, most importantly, fail her.

"I'm sorry, Vail. I'll help with whatever I can. I think vampire Penelope is more powerful than Princess Penelope. She might not cure vampirism, but she's going to rule us all one day," he said as I climbed back up the ladder.

"She already does," I answered without hesitation, emerging back into the chaos.

"I see him! Wow. It's been at least twenty years since I've seen a gargoyle!" Henry knelt before Otto and frowned. "Poor thing needs help."

Otto sat on his rump and whined. His broken wing hung loosely at his side.

"How do you see that?" Fritzi's voice rose to a high-pitched shrill. "You're human now. You're not supposed to see anything magic!"

"I wonder if it's because I was in Morningwood and around vampires for too long." He cast a suspicious glance at me.

"Come here. Let me see your eyes!" Fritzi jerked her husband's hand until he stood nose to nose with her. "It's there." She drew in a breath. "Oh my gosh. You have a teeny-tiny spark, but I see it. I think you're part-genie. Do something and see."

"There's been enough destruction in my office. I'd rather any spell-practicing happen outside." Finn crawled out of the hole and walked toward Henry. "Let me see where Penelope bit you."

I raised my brow at Penelope, but she only returned my curiosity with a shrug and flip of her hair.

"You think her bite gave him powers?" Ian leaned against a wall, crossing one boot across the other.

"Wouldn't that be something? It's not Penelope's blood now. It's her bite!"

Finn met my gaze, but I shook my head in warning. Now wasn't the time to break the news to anyone that we would never have pure, royal sunflower blood again. I had to get Penelope alone before I shattered her hopes for a future.

"She bit me right here." Henry craned his neck and pointed at his wound marks. "I don't feel different though. But I sure can see a gargoyle, that fox that's stinking up the room, and even whatever that mangy thing is over there. Is that a big-ass hamster or what? He smells like he bathed in wine. Sheesh."

"That's a ten out of ten insult, so I'll let it pass." Grump plopped down on his bottom with a flop.

"And he talks!" Henry gasped, covering his mouth with his palm.

"What talks?" Fritzi looked around the room and scratched her head.

Henry shook his head and pointed toward animals she couldn't see.

"It's red, like it's infected. She might have leaked some of her toxin in you. New vamps accidentally do that. They don't know how to control that release." Finn ran his thumb over the bite wounds and stepped back.

"You're saying I can straddle realms now because she poisoned me? Is that all it takes? One feisty bite, and I'm back to the big blue dil—" Henry asked.

"Don't," Fritzi interrupted. "Let's keep your old genie habitat to ourselves. No one needs to know where you came from." She waved him away. "But if Penelope's toxin can turn my husband back to a genie—or at least a half-genie—do you think it would work on humans who have zero traces of magic in their blood too?"

"We can only know through testing," Finn said.

I hurried to Penelope and put my arm around her protectively. "She's not doing any testing for a bit. I think we all need a long rest. The sun's almost up, and we've got to get our energy back." I felt the weight of apprehension leave her shoulders as she nuzzled up against me.

Fritzi clasped her hands under her chin and smiled. "I understand and agree. It's so nice to see her in safe hands. I know you'll take good care of her, Vail," she said, stepping into Penelope and hugging her good-bye. "I'm so proud of you. You're everything I knew you'd be and more."

Penelope pressed her lips together and nodded—a move she'd often performed as a princess to ward off a rush of tears.

"Come on. Elly's waiting." Henry reached for his wife and led her away, stepping over the piles of dead vampires. "And sorry I left these assholes' ashes in your office. But at least I stopped them from blowing the place up and destroying everything! That would have been terrible."

"I'll call you when everything is back in order. I could use a friend to talk to," Penelope called out to Fritzi.

"Always at your service, Your Majesty." Fritzi curtsied before disappearing out the door.

Ian followed behind Fritzi and Henry, announcing he had to search for Drake. Drake's broken leg worried me because he was a vampire who refused to slow down. But after seeing Finn's skills inside his secret lab, I had no doubt my crazed brother could grow him a new one if he needed to.

As soon as they were out of sight, Penelope turned to me and whispered, "She reminds me of Gertie sometimes."

"Me too," I agreed.

Finn rubbed the scar across his brow and busied himself with Otto's wing.

"Let's go to bed. I want to crawl into my nook and sleep," she said, burying her face in my chest.

I buckled at the thought of causing her more pain.

I WAITED until Penelope was snug in my arms before I began to speak my dreadful news. Her skin still held a comforting warmth from the shower, reminding me of the days when she'd felt like sunshine.

"Penelope, there's something I need to tell you." I winced. The back of my head still pounded.

"I already know," she said without looking in my direction. She rolled onto her back, staring at the ceiling.

A wave of despair bubbled in my stomach, rendering me speechless until I could figure out my next move. Her knowledge had caught me off guard and left me in an uneasy state to navigate.

"Are you sure you know what I'm about to tell you?" I asked.

"Yes. I could read it in Finn's face when he saw his office. I knew where he'd stored my blood, and a vampire had smashed that cabinet to pieces. There's nothing left of my *before* ... is there?" She propped herself up onto her elbow.

The weight of the world was etched across her frown, dragging us both down into a pit of misery.

"No. I'm sorry."

"So, no babies. No princess school. No life." Her voice grew weak, trailing off into a soft sigh.

A stab of sorrow centered on my empty chest. Whatever dead heart still lingered in my chest ripped itself in two, breaking what had been left of me.

"We can do more tests with your new blood and figure something out. Maybe your toxin has some type of reaction in it. If it can turn Henry back to his roots, maybe it can turn you back to yours."

I held my arms wide, motioning for her to lay her head on the nook of my shoulder. Ever since she'd told me that was her safe space, I'd become aware of how much she used it. She nuzzled into me in greeting, or when she was frightened, or when we made love. Sometimes, she'd even cuddle me just in passing. My body was the least I could offer her, but she deserved so much more.

"You want me to bite myself?" she asked, lowering her cheek to my chest.

"No. Well, maybe. Who knows? All I know is that your toxin is different. But—and not to sound offensive—your bite isn't everything."

She stayed silent a moment too long, causing me to second-guess my confession.

"Bastard!" She playfully twisted my nipple, lifting the mood.

I let out a squeal. "Hear me out!"

"Explain how my bite isn't the bee's knees, or the pixie's wings, or whatever. Grump's rump! Do tell me how I'm *not* fabulous," she said, perking up into the princess I'd missed.

"You're certainly still dramatic—that's for sure." I bit my lip to keep from smiling.

A mixture of grief and relief bounced back and forth between us while she tapped her fingers across my chest, awaiting my explanation.

"Ahem," I cleared my tightening throat. "In The Cave, I had this moment when I realized you were there.

"At first, when that bastard had stabbed me with the needle, the only thoughts flooding my mind had been horrible ones, like grotesque things and visions of stuff I didn't want to remember. I tried to fight them off. I concentrated as hard as I could on the scent of your hair or the way you'd looked at me that first time you rode the chandelier down to the ballroom floor. You were so proud of yourself, and I was too. I focused as much energy as I could on our first dinner at your cottage and sweet Gertie's cautious smile as she watched our conversation. I think she knew then that I was the one to protect you. She couldn't do it any longer, and now, it was up to me. I believe that's why she felt it was safe to go. No matter how many memories I'd tried to center on, these damn traumatic, unrelenting thoughts had kept assaulting my brain and shaping the good into the bad and the bad into the awful.

"But then I heard your voice, and I sensed your presence. I felt what I thought was your heartbeat again. I didn't know it was mine beating after all these years. But that heartbeat ... your heartbeat, it carried me through. I had this tiny fragment of a moment to make a choice, and both my body and mind were fighting over it. I could end it now, or I could end it later. Life or death. I guess that was the disease working on me. The Crux."

"What did you choose?"

"I chose you." I curled my hand around hers and brought it to my lips.

"Thank you," she whispered, burying her face further into my nook.

"You don't have to thank me. It's what I want. I want you. I don't care if we can't have children or if our future looks a hell of a lot different than we both envisioned. Vampire, human, princess, witch, cursed, diseased zombie ... I don't care what I am as long as I get to be it with you."

She smoothed her hand up my chest and caressed my stubbled jawline. Her touch sent the same familiar spark in my veins as it always did. Even as a vampire, she made me feel alive. We clung to each other in long, comfortable silence before she broke the spell.

"Do you realize, even after your death, you've never stopped being Prince Charming?" She climbed on top of me

135

and leaned down, brushing her breasts against my chest. Her nipples peaked against my skin.

I folded my arms around her, answering with my body while losing myself in deadly royal desire. We spent the morning in sessions of lovemaking or slumbering, filling each other with fresh energy.

CHAPTER NINE

PENELOPE

I ROLLED OUT OF BED JUST BEFORE DUSK AND TIPTOED DOWN the hallway.

After the incident at The Cave, I'd remained in bed for days, avoiding confronting my grim reality. I didn't know what to do now that I had destroyed all my enemies and found myself in a hopeless future. I'd longed for vengeance since Prince Theo had cast me out of Poppycock, but with my lousy luck, I'd become stuck in an unfortunate cycle of catastrophe. With nothing left to conquer, my world had grown quiet enough that I'd finally forced myself to succumb to the dead.

"Can't sleep again?" Mirror Mirror asked as I crossed his path.

I stopped in front of him, pausing to take in my startling reflection. I'd aged like fine wine since moving to Morning-wood. The naive young woman who had stepped into Priscilla's crumbling cottage had emerged from hell like a phoenix from ash. I saw it in the wisdom shadowing my eyes and the way my brows were set in rigid confidence. My golden-flecked hair was streaked almost entirely jet-black—a mark for each death at my hands or for each trauma I'd endured. I never figured it out.

But the most alarming transformation in my reflection was the upturned curve of my mouth. Since Gertie's passing and my turning, I hadn't smiled. But I hadn't worn a frown either. I existed on the edge of both emotions, teetering one way or another but never fully committing.

"You know how it is." I brushed my fingertips over my lips, pinching them to make sure I wasn't caught in a dream.

The last year of my life had bubbled over with despair and misfortune. The only toothy grin I'd offered to battle my situations was fake or forced. But I felt a hint of relief fighting to curl my lips upward. It tugged at the edge of my spirit, clawing its way out. My war was finally over, and I could settle in peace, *if* that was what I wanted.

"I know that you've survived the pits of hell and smashed the patriarchy while you were at it. I don't blame you for a lack of sleep. But you're free to live now, you know. Even in death. You don't have to grow comfortable in chaos. You can just be … in all your glory." Mirror Mirror flashed a vision of a crown atop my head. It was the same crown Theo was supposed to wear on the day he hadn't shown up for our wedding.

"I'm trying to learn how to do that. I toss and turn between a past and future, like I'm stuck in between two terrible moments in my history. But I think I'm beginning to at least see a present now. I just have to remind myself to stay on that path and keep moving forward. I can't bounce back and forth between times I can't change anymore. It nearly destroyed me. I just really want something to look forward to, and I'm not sure what that is now. My royal blood is gone, and with it, the cure for vampirism and my hopes for a future have vanished." I adjusted the collar on my silken periwinkle pajamas, sending a whiff of my godmother's scent in the air. My pajamas still smelled of fresh herbs and tea.

Gertie had gifted them to me when I began to sleep at Theo's palace. She insisted that my frayed flannel gown wasn't princessy enough. I had to agree. To get the man, I had to play the part. At least, that was what my princess school had taught me. When I'd begun to have long overnights and weekends at the winery, I'd made sure to bring my fancy-pants pajamas with me along with a few robes and dresses. That pile of wrinkled clothes was all I had left of the old me. After my home had burned down, nothing had been salvageable.

"You still have a future. It will just look different than you envisioned. You're still worth the world to so many, even without your blood. But you didn't hear that from me. I prefer to keep our relationship on the no-feels level. That way, you can't break my face, and I can't break your dead heart," he said. "Bitch!"

I grinned.

"I had to throw that in for good measure, but look, I got you to crack a smile!" He shimmered my reflection back to me.

I let out a long breath, stretching a wide smile across my face. "Thanks, asshole. I think I'm going to take a walk and check for the first signs of spring. Maybe I can busy myself in the vineyard this season. I don't have a green thumb, but I like to drink."

"And … the princess is still in there," he said in a clipped voice. "Classy."

"Penelope?" Vail peeked from over my shoulder in Mirror Mirror's reflection. He twisted his hands together, rubbing his wrists.

"What're you doing up?" I turned on my heels and bit my lip hard, sucking in a shallow sigh through my fangs.

He was still wearing his gray sweatpants and white tee from the night before. I raked my gaze over his tight body and fought the sudden urge to take him back to bed.

"I know when you sneak out of bed. No matter how stealthy you think you are, I still feel you leave. It's your absence I sense. I just wanted to make sure you were okay," he said, walking toward me and brushing a strand of hair from my face.

"I'm okay. I couldn't sleep and thought I'd take a walk. Maybe see if spring has sprung. I'm over Morningwood winters. In Poppycock, it never grew cold. We had sunshine and rainbows year-round. This miserable weather is wearing me down."

He turned his face to a nearby window. The sun had dipped below the horizon, radiating a warm glow over the treetops and turning the sky purple.

"Would you like some company? We can try to find some signs of new life together. Maybe the bunnies will hop out of their burrows to say hi. Or we can find a bird's nest ripe with eggs. It'll be a little adventure. I'm sure the forest will come alive if you're walking its paths. How about it?" He offered his hand.

I took it without hesitation. "I'd love that."

I waved good-bye to Mirror Mirror and slid my feet into a pair of boots I'd left by the door. Vail tied on his sneakers and stretched. It had been a long time since I'd taken a walk in the woods. I'd busily tried to avoid my old stomping grounds.

"Ready?" He opened the door, sweeping his hand in front of him and letting me pass.

"I think so," I said, peering straight ahead and putting one foot in front of the other, inching inside the forest.

We trudged along the wooded path in silence, leaping over mud puddles and fallen trees. The warmth of the day still lingered enough to cast a toasty comfort against my skin.

"We have visitors," he said, pausing against a rotting tree.

I looked behind me to find Otto, Grump, and Trevor trailing our footsteps. The gargoyle's bandaged wing stuck straight in the air, bobbing behind him as he walked with his friends. Grump, surprisingly, walked in a straight line, as if he were sober. Trevor pounced along, dashing through hollowed logs and tearing mushrooms from the forest floor.

"They're still protecting you, you know. Even though they know you don't need it. You're their mama," he said the words before realizing their weight. A pang of guilt showed in his drooping mouth as soon as he made the blunder.

"I guess I am." I brushed off the brief ache through my chest and continued on the path, staring at the uneven ground to avoid a muddy fall.

Rotting acorns were scattered beneath us, crunching underfoot. When I looked up again, we'd made it to the clearing where I used to practice my spells when Gertie and my friends ran me out of my own home. The tree stump in the middle of the clearing was still softened with a fine layer of moss.

"Do you remember this place?" I asked, stopping at the stump to brush my palm against its top. The fuzzy moss tickled my fingertips, filling me with nostalgia.

"How could I forget? It's the spot I first laid eyes on you. I went for a walk and heard this beautiful sound drifting through the trees, luring me for a closer look. I thought I'd come upon a siren, beckoning me into her deadly spell."

He tilted his head back and looked up. The soft white glow of stars began to appear, sprinkling across a dusky sky.

"In the woods?"

"You never know in Morningwood." He looked back at me and shrugged.

"True." I circled the clearing with my furry friends following closely on my heels.

"But when I snuck closer to you, your voice changed. Instead of the sweet birdsong that had pulled me in, you began to spout out more of a heavy metal melody. I didn't know what to think!"

I stifled a laugh with my palm. "That's because I had this bright idea that I could summon darker things if I sang in a scarier voice."

"And?" he asked.

"I summoned you, didn't I?" I stepped into him, hooking my finger underneath his waistband and pulling him close before I realized my mistake.

His body grew rigid against mine.

"I'm sorry. I didn't mean that you brought me darker things or that you're bad. That came out wrong. I meant that —" I drew back. Guilt washed over me, punching me in the gut.

"I know what you meant," he said, stopping me. "It's okay."

"No, it's not okay. You changed my life. Theo had changed the course of my life, but you … you changed it completely. I'm an entirely different person now. Look at all I can do!"

I waved my fingers in the air and summoned a group of fireflies. They blinked in a heart-shaped pattern before disappearing.

His fangs peeked from beneath a tight-lipped smile.

"You changed mine too. Look what I can do!" He stepped back and spun in a twirl. Nothing happened.

"That … that's an impressive move you got there. Where'd

you learn that one?" I held back a burst of laughter and played along.

"Oh, just from some random dance partner I had once. We counted dance steps by heartbeats. One, two, three. One, two, three, three." He danced around the clearing, stopping back at my feet.

"She sounds fabulous."

"She is."

I looked away, toward the path that led to my old home. "Have you been there since it happened?" I asked.

He followed my gaze and stared into the distance. Nearby, a mourning dove began to coo.

"No. Not since you left." His voice softened.

"Take me there?" I asked, noticing a quickly darkening sky.

A chorus of crickets began to hum, echoing their song throughout the woods. My spine tingled with anticipation.

"Are you sure?" he asked, creasing his brows.

I swallowed hard and reached out for him. "Yes. Just grab my hand, please. I'm not feeling very steady. But I want to see it. I never got to say good-bye."

He dropped his gaze and took my hand, intertwining his fingers with mine. "Let's do it then."

He tightened his grip as we walked toward my cottage. I searched the area for anything I could use as a bouquet or a trinket to lay on Gertie's grave, but the dormant forest floor still showed zero signs of life. My merry band of misfits scurried ahead of us, following an old, familiar path. I paused, breathing in a whiff of soot drifting through the branches. The scent assaulted my memory with the last scene I remembered from that terrible night.

"Are you sure you want to do this? We can turn back," he said, still clinging to my hand.

"We're almost there. I need the closure." I continued down the beaten trail.

Up ahead, I could already see my home's ruins bathed in a paltry moonlit glow. I dropped Vail's hand and picked up my pace. Aside from the cobblestone fireplace, nothing was left, except a thick layer of ash. I kicked through the remains and dropped to my knees.

"Penelope!" Vail rushed to my side, falling down next to me.

"I'm all right. I just ... I don't know what I was thinking, coming here. Seeing it like this and knowing this is where she supposedly saved me!" I threw my hands in the air. "She didn't have to do that. She didn't have to leave me like that. She could have just told me, and we would have figured it out! What did she think would happen to me after she left?"

I tilted my chin up to the sky and bared my fangs. A racking sob hitched in my throat. Vail put his arm around my back, calming the tremors ricocheting off my body and over-taking his.

I clung to him and cried, releasing a pent-up sorrow I'd held on to for far too long. My animals stirred, settling quietly into the dust beside me in an unwavering show of support. Vail remained silent, offering me his bottomless strength after I finally lost all of mine. After all this time, he carried the weight of my misery for the both of us. I didn't need to grow a new family. I already had the best.

I didn't speak again until I could gather my wits about me and find a break in my shameful loss of control.

"I'm so sorry. I guess I thought I'd be stronger than this." I dipped a finger in the ash and traced a star along with my godmother's name.

"You have nothing to be sorry about. You lost your mother. You're allowed to mourn. Take all the time you want.

I'm not going anywhere." He tightened his grip and stubbornly refused to budge.

I melted my body against his and let out a long-drawn-out sigh. Grump nuzzled underneath my arm, Otto wiped tears from his leathered cheek, and Trevor sniffed the ash, sticking his nose an inch into the soot and snorting. He began to paw furiously at the ground, throwing dust behind him in powdered clouds. I wafted my hand in front of my face, coughing out the gritty particles he'd sent flying into my mouth.

"What's he found?" Vail asked, drawing my attention to the fox's digging.

I drew my brows together and crawled a few steps toward him, sticking my hand in the hole he'd created. Something fragile and rubbery sprouted underneath the ash. I brushed the dust away and peered inside.

"Vail!" I shouted. "Look!"

Vail lunged his body forward and sat beside me, looking at what Trevor had found.

"Oh, look! It's a sign of spring. New life. That's a good omen. I wonder what it is. A vine of some sort?" He shoved more dust from the hole, cleaning the area surrounding the sprout.

"No. It's a sunflower." A wave of dizziness gripped my insides.

Trevor began to dig again a few feet away before yipping. I crawled on my hands and knees toward him, raking my fingers through the soot and discovering another sunflower sprout. I fell back on my bottom, wiping a streak of black across my wet eyes before dusting my palms on my dirtied pajamas.

"I don't understand. How can this be? Do you think it's just normal sunflowers?" Vail searched my face for answers.

My animals kicked and dug and brushed away layers of

ash to reveal sprout after sprout emerging through the pile of burned embers.

"No." I rubbed my chest, where my heart would have been hammering with excitement before I turned vampire. But even though there wasn't a heartbeat in my cold, empty chest, I still felt a rush of thrill coursing through my veins. My hopes kindled anew.

"The tips of the two leaves sprouting are tinged with gold. Look closer. We're sitting on a Princess Patch full of sunflowers. I think these are the missing seeds. The ones Gertie stole. These are the ones like me. They have to be." I stood up and stepped off the bed of ruins, motioning for everyone else to stand back.

"Oh my. This is your royal bloodline. This is your family! This is the cure?" His voice squeaked on the last words he murmured.

"This is new beginnings," I whispered.

I summoned a gentle gale of wind and wiped away any remaining traces of ash. The dust floated up into the sky, lifting into a powdery black cloud before drifting away. I sent it back to Poppycock in the form of a raging storm.

"I can't believe this is happening." Vail rubbed a hand over his face and blinked. He paced the ground beside me. "We can have the future we wanted. You can have your school!"

"Or army." I shot a glance in his direction.

His face contorted with unease as he weighed my words.

"I'm not saying an army for battle. Not that type of army. I'm saying an army we build to evolve, not destroy. We can do things differently now," I assured him. "Who says we have to keep the old, traditional ways?"

His shoulders slumped with relief before he broke into a grin as wide as my own. "You're going to make an amazing ruler and an even more amazing mother."

I took a deep breath from habit and stared out over the

dozens of sunflower seedlings sprouting from the ground. Their golden tips sparkled in the moonlight as they turned their leaves toward me in an echo of approval. My furry friends began to play in the distance, fueled by a surge of newfound joy. I shifted on my feet and laughed, finally relaxing into the role I'd waged a treacherous war to gain. I wasn't the same simple princess who had stood here long ago. I'd found my stability and purpose as the Lady of Bostwick even if it came at a hefty price.

I planted my boots firmly into the ground and made a mental vow to raise my future generation of blooms to survive any disaster that plagued them. I wouldn't restrict their knowledge to charms of rainbows, sunshine, or princes to save their day. We were built for so much more. The world was ours for the taking, and I was determined to take it for my children with Vail standing loyally at my side. My death had only been my beginning, and my happily ever after was now my once upon a time.

FROM THE DESK OF FRITZI COX

Dear Reader,

We made it! I'm so glad you took the journey with me back to Morningwood to help our princess earn a well-deserved happily ever after. We survived the adventure together and emerged safely on the other side of the woods. Well done!

I'm happy to report that while I never succeeded in finding a way back to the fantastical realm myself, my husband now balances on the edge of both worlds. He's embraced his new role as translator, of all things, from the other side, so I can continue accurately reporting the supernatural stories you love most. After all, truth is stranger than fiction.

But even without Henry's new abilities, I've gained a helpful group of friends willing to share my passion in reporting. The Bostwick family recently purchased *Starlight Press*, and to my shock and gratitude, Penelope named me editor in chief. We are currently working on releasing our first publication at Abe's Book Emporium and through my newsletter network. These articles and more will be available for your entertainment soon, so please be sure to stop by the bookshop or subscribe to my newsletter today and support the cause!

Along with the growing number of stories piling on my desk, my latest project has been keeping me busier than ever. I'm currently documenting Finn's story as he relates it. The days are long, and the nights are rough, but we are trudging through his tragic past toward a light at the end of his dark tunnel. After learning the nature of his fiancée's death, I understand why he fights so hard for his corpse bride. We are hopeful for his happily ever after even if it might not be the ending he envisions. You can learn more about this love story by continuing on our vampire adventures in my next novel, *Toxic Chemistry*. But as with Penelope's story, it's a deadly gamble, not a charming fairy tale.

Other than news of my thriving business, the only update I have for you is that the brotherhood and my family have grown immeasurably close. The winery has taken care of me and my family, even hosting a recent birthday party for my daughter, Elly. One might think having a child in a den of vampires is the most irresponsible mistake a parent could make, but I trust these beautiful creatures with our lives.

The Lady of Bostwick is adamant on making Morning-wood and the world a better place for every realm. She completely renovated the ballroom into a top-notch school for her upcoming blooms. Her commitment to a peaceful future and growing the next generation of strong, independent princesses has left me in awe. The princess has truly embraced her new role as a vampire queen, and I couldn't be happier to have documented every step of her journey.

I leave you all in good spirits and in a much safer place. From all my exhaustive research, I believe The Council has been completely defeated or any remaining members have fled. You can rest assured that Bostwick has their realm under control. The brotherhood has taken all precautions to secure my business and assure our safety.

Some names and events were altered to protect the innocent, but my tales are hard truths, reported directly from the fantastical.

From Morningwood to the land of the living, this is Fritzi Cox, signing off until we meet again.

EPILOGUE

Somewhere in the Human World

JOSIE

I pulled down the gravel drive and put the pedal to the metal on my big yellow school bus. I was T-minus thirty minutes to being late at a community center clear across the mountains. Tripp had kept me up all night with the ropes—and by ropes, I meant, he'd finally shown me what kinds of tricks a cowboy could perform on bareback. Talk about sore in the saddle! I had to roll out of bed and do a crab crawl right to the shower. It had taken me three cups of coffee and a hot compress before I could stand upright enough to hobble into my bus.

"Long night?" Emma Jean popped up from a seat three rows down, startling me out of my wits.

I swerved the bus, narrowly missing a runaway cow roaming the morning streets.

"What're you doing here so early? How'd you get in here?" I glanced behind me in the rearview mirror.

She sat, twirling her hair and refusing to make eye contact. "Let's just say, I was in the neighborhood."

"You mean, you were at the Miller Ranch. I can only guess which brother you spent the night with."

She didn't answer.

I fiddled with the radio while humming the tune to "Electric Avenue." That damn song had been in my head since I'd made the venture out west. I'd even caught the townsfolk singing it in passing. As a small-town librarian, my words traveled fast.

"Say, do you have any books by Fritzi Cox on this thing? I keep hearing she writes steamy vampire romance, and I, for one, am sick of reading about cowboys. I need a supernatural lover to bite my thigh, not tan my hide. Small-town drama is for the birds." Emma Jean looked over her shoulder at the rows of books secured by straps along the back of my bus's walls.

"You know, now that you mention it, I think I have seen a book by her floating around. Check the Fantasy section when we stop. I think I remember it was a blue book called *Royally* something or other." I cracked my window, letting in the intoxicating scent of gillyflowers and mountain air.

Emma Jean rose from her seat and bounced down the aisle. Her curls bobbed in perfect unison, flowing down her dainty shoulders and trim waist. When people posted their flawless faces on social media and claimed they woke up that way, I knew they were fuller of bull than a young heifer during rutting season. But with Emma Jean, she really did wake up like she'd just won her fifteenth blue ribbon as the county's reigning pageant queen.

I curled my fingers around the steering wheel and rechecked my center mirror. "Emma Jean! You're going to break your neck. Get back here and strap in! You can't go running around the bus like we're not moving. I can't drive while you're up. It's distracting me!"

When I cut my eyes back to the road ahead, the bus hit a large object, rolling over it with a thump. I skidded to a stop, throwing Emma Jean into a nearby seat.

"Oh shit, oh shit, oh shit!" I unbuckled my belt and ran toward the back, helping Emma Jean to her feet before inspecting whose cow I'd just ground to burger.

"I'm all right!" She waved me away. "But whatever you hit isn't. Come on. Let's go take a look."

We hopped out of the door and walked toward the back of the bus. A beautiful woman with hair the color of sunshine crawled out from underneath.

"Oh my gosh! I hit a woman!" I rushed to the woman's side.

Emma Jean followed quickly behind me.

"Are you okay?" I asked, bouncing on my heels in a sickening rush of panic.

I took the woman's arm and pulled her to her feet. She wore a dated dress, as if she'd just stepped out of a silent movie. A rubber tire mark was etched across her blushing face, but I couldn't see any signs of bleeding or trauma on her anywhere.

"Ma'am. Ma'am! Listen to me. You were just in an accident." Emma Jean reached for the woman's shoulders and stooped, staring into her eyes. "Can you understand me?"

The woman shifted her weight. Her joints made a squeaky metal sound.

I scratched my head and studied her. "I think she's in shock."

"She's in something … or on something." Emma Jean took a step back, brushing her palms down her blue jeans.

The woman cracked a broken smile and stuck her thumb in the air. "Ten! Ten!" she said before vanishing in a poof.

Emma Jean and I stared at each other in disbelief.

"Did you just see that? Am I dreaming? Did that really happen? Is this what it feels like to do drugs?" I looked down the desolate road, back and forth, and knelt to peer underneath the bus, but the woman was gone. I shot back up and rubbed my eyes.

"Just add it to the list of reasons I keep running from this crazy town. Douche bags and weirdos—that should be the town slogan. Although I wish I could learn that poof trick. Would have saved me a lot of heartache a time or ten." She turned to leave, heading back into the bus.

I tipped my head toward the sky and whispered a quick thanks that whoever or whatever I'd just smooshed had gotten another chance.

Thank you for reading Princess Penelope and Vail's story! Are you ready to tackle Finn's project and learn about his tragic past? Check out *Toxic Chemistry* and continue with part 2 of the VILF series today!

Sign up for my newsletter to find more information on my latest releases and claim an exclusive e-book for free!

https://kataddams.com/free-book

Join my Facebook group—D.T.F. (Dirty. Tough. Females) —for news, sneak peeks, and more!

ALSO BY KAT ADDAMS

Dirty South Series

Faking Second Chances

Schooling Professor Playboy

Playing Backstage with the Rockstar

Stroking the Boss's ... Ego

Mayday (FREE for Newsletter Subscribers)

DTF (Dirty. Tough. Female.) Series

On the Rox

Cream-Pied

Whip it Out

Just the Tip

FU (FORKS UNIVERSITY FASHION ACADEMY) SERIES

Just Between Us

This Means War

BUCK OFF RANCH SERIES

Josie Thatcher, Cowboy Catcher

Emma Jean, Heartbreak Queen

PARANORMAL ROMANTIC COMEDY

Ghosted

**WRITING PARANORMAL ROMANTIC COMEDY AS
FRITZI COX**

Royally Drained

Royally Cursed

Royally Revamped

Home Sweet Home

Toxic Chemistry

For a complete listing of Kat Addams books, visit

https://kataddams.com

ACKNOWLEDGMENTS

For my little princess. I love watching you bloom! Some days, you're a curious fox, and some days, you're a preteen grump, but either way, you make me proud. One day, you'll rule your own empire, and I'll always be by your side to help. The world is ours for the taking.

Thank you to my amazing editor, Jovana Shirley; my awesome cover designer, Najla Qamber; and my talented graphics designer, Katherine Lopez. Your skills bring my stories to life!

I also want to thank the book community, bloggers, and readers. Your enthusiasm and support keep me going. I appreciate all the reviews, well wishes, and book chatter. It doesn't go unnoticed. DTF!

Lastly, thank you to The D for stepping in and helping me out in the single-mom life, so I can follow my dream and keep writing. You're a ten—ten!—and my *once upon a time*.